"Don't imagine you've stumbled into Camelot."

The warning in David Caradoc's voice surprised Kerry. "I've no idea what you're talking about," she said.

"Of course you have. Look around you. This is my room, my home, my gardens and my estate." David's words were slow and deliberate.

Kerry was a little surprised at the information, but more so by his point in telling her. "Well, that's a rotten deal for Adrian, but I'm sure his paintings sell well."

"Not often enough," David continued. "So, being Mrs. Adrian Caradoc would not be a cushy number."

Kerry's quick temper flared. "You don't think I'm good enough for Adrian!"

David ignored her outburst, and moving toward her, added, "Now you know the score before y̲_____ a̲gain tonight."

D0557200

Jane Donnelly, a former journalist, lives in a picture-perfect cottage just outside Stratford-upon-Avon with her daughter and their assortment of pets. She has written everything from short stories to movie scripts and has developed into a prolific author of warmhearted romance novels since she started to write for Harlequin in 1968. She finds her writer's life immensely satisfying, loves the excuse to travel and still has a reporter's instinct for gathering news and scribbling down notes, which she later uses in her books.

Books by Jane Donnelly

HARLEQUIN ROMANCE

Force Field

Jane Donnelly

Harlequin Books

TORONTO • NEW YORK • LONDON
AMSTERDAM • PARIS • SYDNEY • HAMBURG
STOCKHOLM • ATHENS • TOKYO • MILAN

Original hardcover edition published in 1987
by Mills & Boon Limited

ISBN 0-373-02871-7

Harlequin Romance first edition November 1987

CHAPTER ONE

MAYBE here, thought Kerry Holland as she rattled over the cobblestones of the Cornish town of Penlyn in her yellow Metro bearing the scarlet slogan 'Cotswold School of Motoring'. For the last two months she had been looking for somewhere to buy a house, find a job, and she fancied somewhere by the sea; she had always loved the sea.

The pretty fair-haired girl sitting beside her yelped, 'Hey, look, that's us!' pointing towards a poster in a shop window, and Kerry slowed down so suddenly that the motor-cyclist behind nearly landed on her boot. He hooted furiously and drew up alongside, red-faced under his white helmet, spluttering curses and informing her that she was never going to pass her blankety test.

The car windows were down, it was a warm summer's day—she had been driving slowly through the seaside resort and he should not have been that close—but she looked at him with a beseeching expression, mouthing, 'Sorry', and he muttered, 'No harm done.' Her face was so woebegone that he glanced at the girl in the passenger seat who was holding papers and gasped, 'Cripes, you're not taking the test, are you?'

'No,' said Kerry.

'Well, good luck when you do,' he said and zoomed off, and Louise laughed.

'I like the silly-little-me performance.'

Kerry grinned. She had the mobile features of a born actress: small nose, wide mouth, big, dark eyes that tilted slightly upwards. Her hair was a mop of chestnut curls

5

and she generated the sparks of a restless vitality. 'Nice lad,' she said, 'I didn't have the heart to tell him I passed my test years ago. What did the poster say?'

'I just caught *As You Like It*,' said Louise. 'I'll look out for another.'

There were posters in most of the shop windows. Today was Thursday and on Saturday the town's Flower Festival started, running for two weeks. Kerry and Louise were down here to take part in performances of Shakespeare's *As You Like It* in what they had been assured was a splendid garden. Louise had directions of how to reach the Wayside Guest House where they would be staying and she was following these, while at the same time looking for further mention of their contribution to the festivities.

They found another poster in a less busy road, where they managed to slow down long enough to read that the Stowe Players would be giving *As You Like It* in the gardens of Maen Bos, home of Mrs Erica Caradoc, at 2 o'clock—every afternoon but Sunday from Saturday June 15th. All seats £1.50. Indoors if wet.

'Well, it's either a big house or they're expecting a small audience,' said Louise.

The sun shone in a blue sky and there seemed every hope of outdoor performances, which would be a challenge and a change. The Players had never played outside the confines of their own little theatre before. 'They could be putting us on in the garage,' said Louise, and Kerry grinned.

'In that case, I can see Gerald ordering his troops home.'

Gerald Harris, the producer, who also played the villainous duke, had a strong sense of dignity, which probably came from being a bank manager by profession and getting a lot of deference. Louise worked in a library, and she was here because it promised to be a pleasant holiday.

'Turn left,' she directed. 'Tregunnel Road, that's it. Now look out for Wayside.'

They found the guest house fronting the road. It was bright and white, with colour splashes of hanging baskets and window-boxes of fuchsia and aubretia, and a side drive leading to 'Parking'.

They weren't sorry to get out of the car. They had been travelling since morning, it was almost six o'clock now, and there had been a stream of holiday traffic on the roads. They climbed out, stretching, and breathing in the sea air, which was welcome after the exhaust fumes. 'Looks comfortable,' said Louise, eyeing the guest house.

A middle-aged man came out of the house, florid-faced and smiling. 'Mrs Caradoc's ladies?' he asked and Kerry's lips curved. The description made her think of sleazy belles dismounting from a film stagecoach, bound for the local Wild West saloon. She had an impulse to put her hands on her hips and drawl, 'That's us, stranger.'

'Well, yes,' Louise was saying, and he went round to the boot of the car. 'Welcome to Penlyn,' he said, taking a case in each hand. 'If you'll just follow me.'

The small hall was cool, with chintz-covered armchairs and bowls of flowers. A woman who looked like a shorter edition of the man was behind a little counter. She replaced a phone as they walked in and looked up to smile and wish them good evening and hope they'd had a pleasant journey. At the same time a dog bounded up and past them towards the door they had left slightly ajar. The man called, 'Come back, there,' and Kerry darted to close the door where the dog was standing, irresolute.

'Mustn't he get out?' Kerry asked and the woman smiled again, and sighed while she was smiling. 'Wouldn't do him much good if he did. He's looking for our son and his wife. They left him with us last month. My son's taken a job in Montreal.'

'What's his name?' Kerry asked.

'Richard,' said the woman, and the man smiled.

'She means the dog.'

'Oh, of course,' said the woman. 'Oh, that's Coco. I'm Mrs Hayle, and this is my husband. If you'd just sign.'

They wrote details in the book. The dog looked like a Coco, a clown. He was a gangling mongrel, with long legs, long swishing tail, and short hair mostly white except for an occasional harlequin splash of black. One eye black, and the black markings on the white muzzle looked like a painted grin. He sat in the hall and watched them, and they were not the ones he had hoped they would be.

Kerry could feel for him. She had known how it was to have her family far away. She had been brought up in boarding schools. Coco's family would probably come back for holidays, but she would never see her family again.

She bent to stroke his head and scratch it gently and say softly, 'You're beautiful, do you know that?' He fixed his eyes on her, sad eyes in a clown's face, and Mrs Hayle produced their keys and took them upstairs.

There was almost a sea view. Wayside was not in the harbour, but high on the hill so that some of the bedroom windows looked over roof tops, and below you could see the grey haze of water between the rugged cliffs. 'It's a lovely room,' said Kerry. Again there was chintz on the chairs; here the wallpaper was covered with rosebuds, and there were old fashioned patchwork quilts on both beds.

'We try to make things comfortable,' said Mrs Hayle. 'We like our guests to look on this as home from home. You're actresses, then?'

She sounded impressed and Kerry said, 'Amateurs.'

'Kerry could be a professional,' said Louise. 'We've got a very good little group. I hope you'll come to see us.'

'I'll try, of course, but I'm very busy, we are full,' said Mrs Hayle. 'And, between you and me, I'm not overstruck on Shakespeare; I like something a bit livelier for my money.' She added hastily, 'Not that I'm not sure it'll be very good. Beautiful gardens they are and the weather forecast's fine. Dinner's at seven. Anything you need——' She gestured vaguely downwards. 'Come on Coco, they don't want you getting under their feet.'

The dog had followed them and was sitting, head on one side, for all the world as if he was listening to the conversation. But he made no move and Kerry asked, 'Could he stay?'

'If you don't mind him. Don't let him be a bother.'

'You don't mind, do you?' said Kerry when the door closed.

'Not a bit, he's a nice old thing,' Louise smiled like a pussycat, 'and I won't be in here that much.' Her fiancé was arriving tonight, also booked into Wayside. 'I hope some of them *are* struck on Shakespeare,' she said, 'or we could be playing to the trees. Maybe we should have been doing *The Ghost Train* when Mrs Caradoc came to see us.'

Kerry had opened her case and was hanging clothes on the left-hand side of the wardrobe. 'We couldn't have acted that in the garden, and I don't think she'd have invited us down if it hadn't been something classical. She seemed a very classy lady to me.'

'Didn't she though,' said Louise . . .

In January the Playhouse-on-the-Hill in Stowe-in-the-Meadows had put on *As You Like It*. The theatre had been converted from an old cinema twenty years before and been thriving with an enthusiastic amateur company

ever since. There was a very high standard. You had to
be good to join and there was always a waiting list.

On first nights there were drinks and a buffet supper in
the Green Room for the company and friends who had
been in the audience, and this time the local MP and his
wife had brought a guest along. There were some
striking-looking women there but Erica Caradoc had
stood out, putting even the MP's beautiful blonde wife in
the shade.

She was tall with high cheekbones in a pale face, and a
cloud of black hair. She wore a coat of smoky grey fur
over black velvet and her rings could have been
theatrical props, they flashed so beautifully.

Kerry had never heard of her before but she moved
among them, flanked by the charismatic young MP and
his glamorous wife, like royalty, with a word for all the
cast. She was so appreciative that everybody warmed to
her and it was genuine praise, her eyes glowed while she
was telling them how she had *loved* the play. She *adored*
Shakespeare, she said, and then she had this *marvellous*
idea. Why didn't they come down to Penlyn this summer,
during the two weeks of the festival, and act their play in
her garden?

Colin Clendinnen, the MP, took up the suggestion
from there, declaring that Mrs Caradoc's garden was the
perfect setting for the Forest of Arden, lawns and
spinneys in a natural auditorium. Erica Caradoc offered
to arrange for the players to stay, some at her home, some
with her friends, some in hotels, all as her guests, and she
still expected to make a healthy profit for charity.

Holiday dates were checked. Some could take two
weeks off, some could manage a few days, and before
Mrs Caradoc went back to Cornwall at the end of the
week she had the Players on her list and the promise of a
full cast for all performances.

Kerry had said yes right away. In January she had
foreseen no problems in being away from there for two
weeks in June. All it would need was a little planning to
keep everything running smoothly. She hadn't known
then how the routine of her life was to shatter. In January
she had happily agreed to spend two weeks in Penlyn
pretending to be Rosalind in Mrs Caradoc's garden, and
lately everyone had said that a seaside break could do her
nothing but good.

Louise was here for the fortnight too. She was Celia,
and Orlando was arriving later tonight: Robin Burke,
trainee solicitor whose ring Louise wore, and who was
the reason Louise was getting out a new dress for the
evening.

There were six bedrooms and three bathrooms. The
girls dashed, one after the other, into the nearest
bathroom for a quick shower, and then Louise made
herself scented and seductive in a white halter-neck
dress, and Kerry got back into jeans and a clean T-shirt.

Louise was carefully flicking style back into her fair
hair with a heated brush while Kerry brushed the travel
tangles out of her own hair vigorously. Tomorrow would
be time enough to bother about styling it. Right now she
left it riotous because she planned an early night, coming
back to this room and going to bed with a book. She had a
thriller with her, all quick-moving action to hold her
interest without making her think. She didn't want to
think.

'Ready?' said Louise when her hair was finished to her
satisfaction.

'Sure. How about you, Coco?' Coco padded downstairs with them and went off down a corridor towards
the smell of food.

'Dinner time for him too,' said Kerry.

There were a few empty places in the dining-room.

Guests already seated gave the girls curious glances.
Most of them had been taking their meals together all
week and were interested in newcomers.

They made an attractive pair, Louise very feminine
with her smooth bare shoulders and baby-doll face, and
Kerry, slim-hipped and long-legged, almost boyish.
Louise had spent time on her make-up, but tonight Kerry
had settled for moisturiser and lip-gloss, and Louise got
most of the attention.

Louise did most of the talking too. As a passenger she
hadn't been tired by the journey, and some time soon
Robin would be arriving. He was being dropped off by
another couple, and as he and Louise had only just got
engaged and were planning an October wedding this
would be like a honeymoon. Well, almost.

Louise beamed happily at everyone who caught her
eye, and Kerry let her chatter on, eating her own meal
and putting in the occasional word. Louise was so sure
about her own future: Robin and a house in the new
development on the outskirts of their home town.

That house was rarely out of her mind, she was on the
lookout for anything, from colour schemes to wallpaper
and furniture that she might use in it. Wayside was fresh
and pretty and Louise admired the lace-edged table-
cloths, and the corner cupboard with its collection of
china figurines. Louise had started to collect pink lustre
herself, and a corner cupboard would be just the place to
display it. 'We could have a corner cupboard in the
lounge,' she mused.

'Mmm,' said Kerry.

'Isn't it fun, moving into a new house, thinking how
you're going to have it?' said Louise. 'Aren't you getting a
bit excited yourself?'

Kerry shrugged and Louise said, 'It isn't quite the
same, I know.' She realised that she had been tactless and

almost changed the subject, 'I'm looking forward to seeing Mrs Caradoc's home. That must be a fantastic place.'

'Oh, it is,' said the girl who was serving them with apple tart and Cornish cream. 'It's big enough to be a hotel.'

Four of the cast were staying there, and tomorrow all the Players were meeting at Maen Bos for a rehearsal in the gardens before Saturday's opening.

'How do we get to it?' Kerry enquired, and the girl described the way, rattling off the names of roads and giving them the extra information, 'Mrs Caradoc used to be an actress herself, you know.'

They hadn't known, but it explained the invitation to put on a play in her garden. The name Erica Caradoc rang no bells for Kerry.

'What was she in?' asked Louise, and the girl looked blank,

'I don't know, but she was an actress. Do you want cream?'

She had looked theatrical. It was easy to imagine her in all sorts of dramatic roles, and Kerry was looking forward to seeing her again.

'I wish Rob could have got here in time for dinner,' said Louise, suddenly and wistfully. 'Apple pie's his favourite.'

Kerry didn't want to be around when Robin arrived. Even if there were others in the lounge Louise and Robin could do without Kerry standing by. The others were strangers, no notice need be taken of them, but Kerry would have to be included in their talk, she would be an intruder. Besides, although she was happy for them, their togetherness would emphasise her own loneliness, and she was lonely these days. Not least because she was rootless and without plans. Right now her future was a void. After the next two weeks she hadn't a clue what she would be doing.

Coffee was served in the lounge and after a quick cup Kerry stood up. 'I'm going to look around the town, go down to the harbour.'

'We might see you down there,' said Louise. She had taken a window-seat and was watching the road for the grey Rover that would be bringing Robin.

The evening was cooling although the sun was still shining and Kerry slipped on a denim blouson jacket, then came out of Wayside and ambled through the narrow streets, looking at the houses, the hotels, the shops.

She passed an estate agent's and scanned the cards with their photographs in the window. She could afford one of the terraced houses, and here in the summer there would always be a bed and breakfast trade. But she had to earn a living for the rest of the year and there might not be much scope for that here.

She made her way down to the harbour, which was picture-postcard pretty, with cliffs rising high around it and boats drawn up on the shingle. Holidaymakers in bright summer clothes sauntered in the sunshine, most of the shops were still open and Kerry sat on a low wall, looking over the sea.

This would be a very different place in the winter. No tourists but probably the artists would still be here. One shop with a good corner position on the harbour was the Caradoc Galleries. That was closed, but she had looked at the paintings in the windows and there had been several storm scenes among them that didn't look at all like this calm and peaceful evening.

Lights were on. Through the glass panels of the door she could see more pictures and, in the shop, sculptures, and placed centrally on a pedestal a bronze head that seemed to be glaring straight at her. It was a particularly powerful piece, so much so that she nearly took a step backwards. Then she almost pressed her nose to the glass squinting at it. Who the heck are you? she wondered.

Erica Caradoc was the widow of David Caradoc, who had been a sculptor. Maybe this was her gallery and that was his work. Maybe that was the late David Caradoc. Pity I'm not an artist, Kerry thought. If I were, I could buy a little house down here and join the artists' colony. Standards and styles seemed to vary. Although she was no critic, some of the paintings looked better than others, and she gazed quizzically at three dark blue spheres on a pale blue background and thought, I wouldn't call that a work of genius, before she strolled over to the harbour wall.

It was pleasant here, watching the sun set. Her boarding-school had been on the coast, and she had looked out to sea then because her father was overseas. She had dreamed dreams beside the sea, acting them in her head. For a practical, highly capable girl, she dreamed a lot of dreams.

She had no fears for her future. She was more than able to look after herself, and very soon she would set about organising her life, but the next two weeks she would enjoy playing Rosalind and being beside the sea for the Flower Festival.

Mrs Caradoc's garden sounded lovely. She couldn't wait to see it tomorrow. Well, she could of course, although there was no reason why she shouldn't make her way to the house now, and look through the gates or over the wall or through the hedge. Then she could go back to Wayside.

She remembered the directions. It was right up the steep main road, and then a few more twists and turns. Higher than Wayside, up on the cliff top, and when she reached the gates dusk was falling. They were black wrought-iron gates, high and big and open. A wide drive curved away to the right and on the left were gardens. She walked through the gates and after a few steps she could see the shape of a house through the trees but it was the garden she wanted to see. A lawn was skirted by a hedge and dotted on the lawn were four great rocks. Rocks that had been got at. Smoothed here and there and the occasional hole bored through. In the fading light they reared over her as she wandered around viewing them from all angles. If these were Erica's husband's work he had gone in for his art in a big way, and if this was going to be the Forest of Arden it would be like acting in Stonehenge.

There were archways in the hedge, and she walked through one and suddenly everything was quiet. Probably it was quiet before and she hadn't noticed, but beyond the arch of the beech hedge a hush seemed to fall on her. This was another lawn. No rocks here, a few trees, and at the far end steps leading up to a circular white-pillared summer house that would be a perfect background for the court scenes. This would make a fantastic outdoor theatre.

She walked across the soft springy turf to the white steps. It would be so easy to slip into the spirit of Rosalind here. Trees backed the arbour, a spinney, nearly a wood, and in the failing light it was magical. She was almost holding her breath because they were surely here in the wood with her, Celia and Orlando and all the motley crew.

She moved like a shadow. This was the Forest of Arden and she was Rosalind, and when the house loomed up she turned away, and it vanished because there should have been no house there, only trees. She was standing by a horse chestnut tree with great thick boughs, and she climbed up into it, agile and supple, sitting among the leaves gloating over what was for now her kingdom.

They couldn't act in the wood, of course, but on the fringe, and knowing it was here would make everything real. She ran through some of her lines in her head and the sensuous music of the words made her feel as if stroking fingers were running up and down her spine.

She was high on fantasy, living, breathing Rosalind. When she jumped down, she landed lithely, and stood for a moment, playing the boy. 'Were it not better, because that I am more than common tall, that I did suit me all points like a man?' She swaggered a little, squaring her shoulders, hands on hips.

Then she heard a twig snap and a man stepped out of the shadows, big and dark and menacing, coming towards her. Fantasy faded and terror erupted and she turned and ran, certain of nothing except that he meant her no good.

He was running too, she could hear him behind her, and when he grabbed her she knew real fear. All her instincts on panic alert she swung a clenched fist into the face that was glaring down at her. She felt the impact numb her whole arm, and it made him loose her, and then they were struggling in earnest and she thought wildly, if I get out of this I'm taking up karate, and fought as if it was for her life and for all she knew it could be.

She didn't have the time or the breath to scream until he had pinned her down, his weight on top of her and then she tried desperately to gulp in enough air to scream and heard him say, 'You're a girl,' sounding astonished and surprising her so that she let out the little air she had managed to get into her lungs. 'You don't fight like a girl,' he said.

This put a different slant on things. She panted, 'Had a lot of experience fighting girls have you? Who are you?'

'David Caradoc,' he said, and she heard herself gasp idiotically,

'But you're dead.'

He was no longer on top of her. He had almost loosed her, if you didn't count a grip like iron on one arm, but she was still too punch drunk to do more than sit up groggily demanding, 'What's your game?'

'What's yours?' God, he looked grim. 'You went in through that upstairs window, didn't you?'

'What upstairs window?' What *was* he on about?

'I saw you jump from the tree,' he said. 'What have you got?' He started to frisk her, hands going into her pockets, and that brought her scrambling to her feet as she squirmed away spitting,

'Get your hands off me, you great ape. I haven't been into the house. I'm an actress. I'm playing Rosalind here on Saturday. I was getting the feel of the place.'

'One of Erica's strolling players? Then why did you run?'

'Lord knows.' If it hadn't been dark she wouldn't have done. If she hadn't been on another plane and he hadn't scattered her wits materialising like that. 'When you came crashing out of the undergrowth I panicked.' He hadn't crashed. It was the sudden shock that did it. She swallowed, 'I thought you were going to attack me; I could end up raped.'

'You flatter yourself.' He grimaced and winced, she had caught him a cracking blow with that first swing. 'You make a very believable young thug,' he said, 'but I can't see you as the sweetest rose.'

'Oh, you do know your Shakespeare?' She was stung into sarcasm but not capable yet of a cutting retort because her head was buzzing like a swarm of bees.

'Are you all right?'

'Of course. Never better. I always feel fantastic after a really good fight.'

'You'd better come into the house,' he said as she brushed herself down with little flicking touches. She was going nowhere with him, although she needed to go somewhere and examine her bruises.

'No, thank you,' she said tartly. 'I've had enough Caradoc hospitality for one night.'

She strode off and he let her go and she made her way fairly steadily to the lawn with the rock sculptures and through the gates. One thing that David Caradoc wasn't was dead, therefore he had to be another Caradoc. Son maybe, only from what she could see of him in the near darkness he looked older than his mother.

He could have marked her face just now; he could have knocked her teeth out. That was lucky, and now for the bad news. He had given her the fright of her life and she could well be black and blue tomorrow, painting out bruises all over.

By the time she reached Wayside, breathing very deep all the way, she had steadied down. There were several people in the entrance foyer and Mrs Hayle greeted her with, 'Had a nice walk?'

'Thank you,' said Kerry, 'it was most interesting.' At the sound of her voice the dog came out of the lounge and Mrs Hayle said, 'I do believe he's been waiting for you.'

'Don't jump up,' Kerry begged. 'You could well knock me down.' She scratched behind his ear again and asked. 'May I take him up to my room?'

'If you want to,' said Mrs Hayle. 'He has taken a fancy to you. He's been really lost since they left him here.'

Louise and Robin were sitting in a high-backed two-seater sofa in the lounge. On a small table in front of them was a bottle of sparkling wine with which they had been toasting each other. As Kerry passed the open door

Louise spotted her and waved a glass. Kerry smiled and indicated, 'I'm going up.'

Louise beckoned but Kerry headed for the stairs and was leaning on the dressing-table, examining her face in the mirror, when Louise followed her in. 'Aren't you coming down for a drink?' Louise asked. 'It's our second bottle, there's plenty left.'

'I don't think so.' It was a relief to find she was unmarked, she couldn't have sworn he hadn't hit her face. She continued to scrutinise it, frowning, and Louise peered over her shoulder at her reflection, and wanted to know,

'What's the matter? Why are you scowling?'

'I got into a fight,' said Kerry. Louise's rosy lips fell open in horror and Kerry went on, 'I walked up to the Caradoc house to look at the garden. That's marvellous by the way, couldn't be better if it had been designed for the play. There's a sort of wood there too and I walked through that and climbed up a tree. Well,' Louise's eyebrows had risen, 'it was there and it was a nice tree. Anyhow when I jumped down it was nearly dark and suddenly this man appeared, very big, and I panicked and ran. And he ran after me and when he grabbed me I hit him, and that was when the fight happened, which he won, I suppose. He'd thought I'd been breaking into the house, there must have been an open window. If I'd explained at the beginning instead of running it wouldn't have happened, but he thought I was a man.'

He thought she had none of the attractions of a girl, and she said with satisfaction, 'I'm glad I blacked his eye; I'll bet I did.'

Louise didn't know whether to laugh or not. 'Who was it?'

'A David Caradoc.' Kerry sat down on the stool. 'She is a widow, isn't she, so I don't know who he is.'

'I do,' said Louise promptly. 'Mrs Hayle's been telling us.' Louise loved knowing things. She was always a mine of gossipy information. 'That was David Caradoc's son. The first Mrs Caradoc died ages ago, Erica was the second wife and her son is Adrian Caradoc.'

'Definitely it was David I had the fight with,' said Kerry.

'You picked the big man.'

Kerry pulled a face. 'I shouldn't think they come much bigger.'

'Well, it's young Adrian and Mr Caradoc,' Louise elaborated. 'And Mr Caradoc is the name that carries the weight around here so from now on you'll know, won't you.'

She had decided that Kerry's adventure had its comic side and she giggled. 'You've made a fine start with the family; do you think he'll come and watch the play?'

'Doubt it.' Kerry shrugged and smiled too. 'He said he thought I'd make a lousy Rosalind.'

'Cheek!' Louise yelped. 'Well, if he does come he'll know different. Sure you're OK?'

'Quite sure.'

'I've got to tell Rob about this,' said Louise and went off smiling.

Coco was lying on a rug, head cocked again as though he had been listening to every word, and Kerry said, 'Now let's see the damage.' She removed her jacket and T-shirt and looked at herself, in the flesh and in the mirror. Her shoulders, where he had pinned her down, were tender and there were distinct fingerprints on her arm. It was lucky she didn't bruise easily, and that the denim jacket had given her some protection.

Glaring at her reflection, she could see what he meant about her making a believable thug; she looked like a tough young tearaway. But she knew how to project a charge of sensuality, and she amused herself by doing just that, smouldering into the mirror, lids lowered, lips parted. If he was in the audience when the players gave *As You Like It* she would show him if she could play Rosalind.

She had always enjoyed acting. Even now she identified with the heroine of every book she read, and at school she had played parts in her head whenever she was lonely. Her father was in the army, and most of her school holidays had been either with friends or sometimes staying on at school, alone except for a skeleton household staff.

She had been the leading light of the school dramatic society and drama was the subject she had wanted to study afterwards, but her father had said, 'Take a secretarial course first. Acting's a tricky profession. When you've got some other qualifications then we'll think about it.'

Kerry couldn't remember her mother, who had died when she was four, but she had always adored her father. She would do anything he wanted and so she had taken the secretarial course. She was eighteen and he had retired from the army that year, bought a house and started a driving-school, and she had begun doing his clerical work and running his home.

Acting was a hobby now, tremendous fun and a marvellous escape. She had been with the Players for four years, and it was a democratic company where everybody did everything, so that she had been stage-hand as often as star, behind the scenes as well as behind the footlights. But it was accepted by them all that Caroline Holland—whom everybody knew as Kerry—had a blazing natural talent.

Coco was like an audience. He listened while she told him that she intended to be the sexiest Rosalind ever, so that the man who had knocked her flat tonight would come up afterwards speechless with admiration. No, she wasn't that big-headed, and neither was she a professional, but she *could* act and it would be highly gratifying if she could make him admit that.

'You think I'm an OK Rosalind, don't you?' she asked Coco who thumped his tail and grinned.

Even if she wasn't bruised she could be stiff tomorrow. That fight must have been equivalent to a killing workout, and Rosalind was an athletic girl, it wouldn't do for her to be hobbling around. A hot bath might help to loosen the muscles, and Kerry poured a liberal dose of herbal salts into the water and soaked for a few minutes telling herself how much good this was doing. Then she dried herself gently, dabbing rather than rubbing, and came out of the bathroom in a white towelling robe to find Coco lying just outside.

He did seem to be adopting her. Perhaps no one had fussed him since his owners emigrated, perhaps he liked being talked to, and she found the contrast betweeen the grin of his mask and the mournfulness of his eyes rather endearing.

When she got into bed he settled down on the rug. 'If they want you,' she said, 'they'll come and get you. I hope you don't snore.'

She tried to read her book, but tonight it couldn't hold her. Her thoughts kept drifting back to the garden of Maen Bos. Until David Caradoc turned up it had been like an enchanted wood. In daylight the mystery would be less of course, but it was something special and it was exciting to think that it would be her stage for the next two weeks.

She wished she had stood her ground and kept her head. As Louise said, she had made a fine start with the Caradoc family. She wondered how Erica had reacted to the story when David went into the house and said, 'I've just met one of your strolling players, a very excitable girl.'

And Adrian. She wondered about Adrian. 'Young Adrian' to the locals, according to Mrs Hayle. A schoolboy? A young man? A younger edition of David? She wondered what David looked like when he wasn't glaring.

All she could recall of him was a large and angry man. Although as she lay in the darkness re-living the scene, she remembered his face after the confusion of the struggle when he had loosed her. Strong, hard, maybe interesting as faces went. The hostility that was still sharp between them had probably heightened her perception because now she was surprised how much she could remember about him, considering her head had been swimming and it had been dark.

Tomorrow she would see the gardens again and possibly David Caradoc. In daylight he might be a nice ordinary guy, smaller than she remembered.

Much later Louise crept into the room but Kerry, who was a light sleeper, heard her and raised herself on an elbow. 'Hey Celia, are you playing around with Orlando?'

'Good night, sweet coz,' Louise gurgled and Coco growled softly and Louise squealed, 'Is that that dog?'

'Well, it's not me,' said Kerry. 'Do you mind?'

Louise didn't. There wasn't that much left of the night anyway, and she got into her own bed yawning.

'Did she say what David Caradoc did for a living?' Kerry asked casually.

'The one you had the scrap with? He's another sculptor.'

'There are rock sculptures in the garden,' Kerry reflected. 'Huge great things, I don't know what they're supposed to be. I wonder which one did them.'

Louise didn't know but Louise was intrigued. 'Are you interested in him?'

'Idle curiosity,' Kerry murmured. 'We didn't exactly take to each other.'

Her shoulder ached when she shifted in her bed, and she hoped that his eye was smarting.

CHAPTER TWO

LOUISE was still asleep when Kerry got out of bed next morning and slumbered soundly while Kerry spent five minutes exercising. Nothing noisy, just some stretching and pushing, checking that her body had recovered from last night's punishment. There were a few bruises but she was relieved to find that she could twist and turn, bend low and stretch high, without a twinge; and when she came out of the bathroom she went across to Louise's bed, leaned over her and asked, 'Are you skipping breakfast?'

Louise squinted up from under heavy lids and mumbled, 'Wasser time?'

'Ten to nine.'

Louise groaned. 'I said we'd be down at nine.' She rubbed her eyes and rolled out of bed, staggering towards the washbasin in the corner, and there was silence while Kerry put on her make-up and a white cotton shirt dress with a broad red belt, and scarlet sandals, cord-tied around her ankles.

Louise moved fast, grumbling about it being worse than getting up for going to work, but by the time she was brushing her hair she was cheerful and she went downstairs smiling at everyone she met. Especially at Robin, who was sitting at their table reading a morning paper.

Robin Burke was an amiable young man, given to bursts of schoolboy humour. As the girls reached the table he asked, grinning, 'What's all this about you attacking strange men?' putting up his hands in mock defence.

'Don't worry,' said Kerry, 'I never hit a man wearing glasses.'

Rob's horn-rimmed glasses gave him a studious air. When he took them off he looked less imposing but he rarely did take them off because he was very short-sighted. This morning, with the sun shining outside and the holiday just starting, his eyes twinkled behind the gleaming glass of his spectacles. 'Morning darling,' he said and kissed Louise. 'Sleep well?'

'She slept like a log,' said Kerry. 'For all of three hours.'

'Don't tell me you waited up,' said Rob.

'Never closed my eyes till she came in.'

'Mind you, she wasn't alone,' said Louise, and that took Rob aback.

'I've made a very good friend,' said Kerry. 'We've got a lot in common,' and they gave their breakfast order and drank some of their coffee before they explained to him that the very good friend was a dog.

The Flower Festival was starting tomorrow but that afternoon Robin and the girls walked to Maen Bos through a town that was putting up bunting and flower arrangements. Everywhere was bustling with anticipation. The air smelled of flowers, wafts of perfume came at them, and Kerry felt almost carefree. Louise, hand in hand with Rob, watched her friend with satisfaction. It was good to see Kerry smiling. This had been a bad time for her, and Louise felt that the two weeks ahead could be a real saver.

They had spent the morning on the beach, lunching outside a quayside restaurant, and now they were on their way to a rehearsal of *As You Like It*.

Having walked to the house last night Kerry knew the

way. She had described the gardens to them but they were still impressed when they reached the gates. 'It's a ruddy great park,' Rob exclaimed and at that moment a car hooted and turned, the four inside waving.

More of the company: Sandra and Den, husband and wife hairdressing team, William, a young farmer and Jeremy, who played Touchstone and worked in a menswear shop. 'See you,' they called as the car went on down the wide curving drive.

'The house is that way,' said Kerry. 'The gardens where we shall be acting are beyond that hedge.'

The hewn rocks looked much the same as they had last night, very big. 'Were those what you were talking about?' asked Louise.

'Makes a change from garden gnomes,' said Rob flippantly, and Louise grimaced.

'I wouldn't like them in my garden.' One of them would have left very little room in the patch behind Rob and Louise's new home, and Rob grinned.

'We'll stick to the gnomes. Hey, look at this. How the other half lives.'

The house was built of mellow grey Cornish stone. Green Virginia creeper covered the first floor, another two storeys rose above with gable windows in the roof. It was a splendid house, set in fantastic grounds. No wonder Erica Caradoc swanned around like royalty, thought Kerry, living in a place like this. She said, 'You know, I'm looking for a new house, well, I think I could settle for this one.'

'A really neat little place,' Louise joked as they walked towards an open door. There was no sign of the car in the forecourt but the four were in the hall, and as Kerry and Robin and Louise appeared in the doorway a woman called in high twittering tones,

'More actors? Splendid. Do come in.'

A staircase curved up to a gallery. The hall seemed immense, and the woman was small and birdlike, with bright eyes and short dark hair smooth as feathers to her head. She hopped around, drawing them into the house, ushering them all towards another open door.

'I'm Penelope Penrose,' she said. 'Do call me Penny, I'm a member of the festival committee for my sins, and I do think this is a super idea of Erica's and I think it's splendid of you all to come, and I know we're going to make lots of money.'

The other players were sitting around in a drawing-room, where sunlight streamed through long windows on to walls with the patina of silk. The furniture was Georgian with the elegance of a bygone age, and Kerry would have loved to walk around and examine things, pick up ornaments, peer at pictures. Her eyes flickered. All the faces were familiar; David Caradoc was not here, but Erica Caradoc came forward, hands outstretched to welcome them.

In sunlight she looked older, but her skin was smooth and there was no silver in her dark waving hair. She made a dramatic picture in a silk kingfisher-blue dress that clung and flowed. 'Isn't this *lovely*? Aren't we *lucky* with the weather?' There was a murmur of assent all round, and Erica turned to Gerald, 'Are we all here now?'

Gerald and Ruth, his wife, were staying at Maen Bos, so were Jenny and Griff, another couple. Gerald as producer had been allocated the theatre-house but with Jenny and Griff it had been the luck of the draw, and the four of them were plainly revelling in their luxurious lodgings. Gerald, middle-aged and comfortably built, looked completely at home, sitting well back in a Sheraton armchair holding his clipboard and viewing his company.

I'm glad my number didn't come up for staying here, thought Kerry. It is a perfectly splendid house but I wouldn't want to spend a fortnight under the same roof as David Caradoc. Even this place might not be big enough for both of us.

Gerald got up. 'All present and correct.'

'Then we'll show them around shall we?' said Erica, and she led the way back into the hall. 'If the weather had been foul,' she said, 'we could have put on the play in here.' She waved a gesturing arm. 'Opened doors and brought in some of the plants from the conservatory. Of course the numbers would have been restricted, but we have had plays in here.'

Kerry could see how the hall of Maen Bos would make a lovely little theatre, using the stairs and the gallery. 'I used to be an actress,' said Erica, 'and you never lose the feel of the theatre, do you?'

This was news to most of them, and somebody asked, 'What parts did you play?'

'So many,' she gave a wistful little smile, 'but so long ago.' Her gaze lighted on Kerry. 'You're Rosalind, aren't you? I remember you.' And Kerry wondered if it was her Rosalind that Erica remembered or whether last night's performance was on her mind. But Erica was on her way and they followed in a little crowd at her heels.

Stables and garages were at the back of the house, with trees beyond, and then the moors, merging mistily on the skyline. They walked through the spinney that Kerry had explored, and with sunlight filtering through the leaves it was even lovelier, she thought, and then they reached the long lawn with the arbour.

'Here we are,' said Erica, and stood back, smiling and silent. So did the four who were staying at the house and had seen it already. The rest were ecstatic because it was such a perfect setting and they were going to have a great time, acting their play here. One of the archways in the hedge led to a marquee that had been set up as changing rooms, and Erica led them through to that. 'There's a tennis court,' she pointed out. 'Use that any time you like, of course, and there's the studio'.

A grey stone building stood alone. 'You must meet David, my son,' she said, 'well, my stepson.' And Kerry's immediate reaction was to stay where she was. She had met David Caradoc and she doubted if he was anxious to renew the acquaintance, but Louise grinned at her and murmured, 'Come on,' when she hung back, and after that she could hardly turn away.

Nobody else hesitated. Erica tapped on a door and opened it and they all followed her in as though this was part of a sightseeing tour, and Kerry felt she should be warning them that David Caradoc disliked intruders. But Erica seemed sure of a welcome for them all and Kerry—propelled by Louise—crept in, and stood at the back of the semi-circle that had formed just inside the doorway.

Daylight hadn't diminished him, he was a big man. In the darkness he had been grey but in daylight he had dark reddish hair, eyes of a piercing electric blue, and a tanned skin. He looked up from a lump of clay on which he was working, facing them.

Erica was gaily introducing them all: names and roles, she knew what they were all playing, and he was listening with what appeared to be courtesy. Kerry had been right about the face, it was strong, and she watched the mouth when he smiled and thought, the smile's like Coco's, it doesn't reach his eyes. And then, yes it does, he's finding this amusing. So what's funny? The strolling players? The way everybody's grinning and nodding?

When Erica said, 'And Kerry, who is Rosalind,' she looked at him unsmiling, and there was a mark on his cheek; and he said,

'I must apologise for last night.'

That was a lovely line. That swivelled every head towards Kerry and she began to stammer her explanation, 'I came into this garden last night and he thought I was a prowler and there was—well, a sort of scuffle.'

Louise gave a yelp of smothered laughter while everyone else went on gasping and gawping. 'Oh *dear*,' said Erica and either this was the first she had heard of it or she was a good actress. She sounded astounded. 'Well, of course,' she went on, 'there have been break-ins. Only last month one of our friends left a window open and——' She gave a puzzled little laugh. 'But you don't look anything like a prowler.'

'It was getting dark,' Kerry admitted. And last night's clothes could have passed for a boy's. Today she was every inch a girl. She laughed, making it throaty and provocative. 'I didn't mind that too much, but when I said that I'd come to play Rosalind he said he couldn't see me in the part, so I feel the least he can do is turn up and watch.'

She was determined he should. He was not impressed by them so far, calling them Erica's strolling players in that dismissive fashion as though they were third-raters. Or perhaps he was like Mrs Hayle and couldn't stand Shakespeare. Ruth leapt to her defence, urging, 'Of course you must come, Kerry's a terrific actress. She's the only one in the company who can weep on cue. Kerry can have tears rolling down her cheeks if a role calls for it.'

'So can most children,' said David Caradoc drily.

'Maybe actors are children at heart,' said Kerry. 'Like most artists.'

As she spoke she was aware of a bronze model of a rearing horse on a shelf, fashioned with superb skill, and knew there was nothing childlike about this artist.

'I shall look forward to your first performance tomorrow,' he told them, 'and now, if you will excuse me.' That was enough to have them all filing out, because it was said with the quiet authority of someone whose orders were rarely questioned. The big man round here . . . the name that carries weight . . .

Not with me, thought Kerry, churning with inner rebellion. You are giving no orders to me.

In the girls' section of the marquee there was a long bench and a trestle table, a full-length mirror and several table-top mirrors in which they could fix their hair and make-up. Ruth Harris was a very efficient wardrobe mistress and the costumes hung on a rail. The clothes were simple, the changes few. The men wore dark pants, with frilled shirts and velvet jackets for the court scenes. Rosalind and Celia had flowing dresses and jewelled circlets in their hair for the court and the wedding, and Celia wore a floral print in the forest of Arden where Rosalind was in dark trousers and a white shirt.

The dress rehearsal this afternoon was less concerned with acting their lines than learning where they would be standing when they said them. Gerald had already worked out his choreography. He positioned them on their marks, and pointed out the microphones and warned them of trailing cables, and the sunshine and the open air had them all in high good humour. When Kerry had rattled through the epilogue and they were all bowing to the empty stretch of lawn where the audience would be, Louise said happily, 'Isn't it a lark? Aren't we going to have fun?'

'Nothing surer,' said Kerry and thought, nothing is sure. Except that tomorrow she would show David Caradoc that she could play Rosalind. That, at least, she was almost certain about.

After the rehearsal the company split. Kerry had

several offers but she went her own way, back down to the harbour again, and took another look into the Caradoc Galleries. The open sign was on the door today and she wandered in. Several other holiday-makers were looking around and watching them all was a young woman about Kerry's age with a supercilious expression and a weary air. Kerry wondered if she was there to help the customers or to stop shoplifters stuffing small articles into beach bags. She didn't look as though she trusted anybody she could see.

The head was still on its pedestal and this was what was intriguing Kerry because she felt now that it probably was the present David Caradoc's work. She walked up to it and it had a power you could feel, like the build-up of atmosphere before a storm. When the young woman walked past her she asked, 'Who is it?'

'A tin-miner,' said the girl.

'No name?'

'No.'

'How much?' said Kerry. The girl hadn't turned to address her, nor was she going anywhere in particular, just moving vaguely around. Now she said scornfully, as if she was talking to someone who was wasting her time, 'It isn't for sale. David Caradoc's work is commissioned or sold as soon as it goes on the market.'

'Oh well,' Kerry drawled, 'I don't think I like it very much,' and that made the girl stop and frown. 'I don't think it would be comfortable to live with,' said Kerry, upstaging her superior air, 'and life being what it is I feel I must have beauty around me.'

She swept from the shop, and went climbing the rocks as far out as she dared, and sat on a crag and watched the sea. She wasn't sure why she had wanted a closer look at that piece of sculpture, just idle nosiness maybe, as she had told Louise last night, but she was curious about the man.

Coco was now taking it for granted that he stayed with her most of the time she was in Wayside. Louise and Rob had gone off for the rest of the day so Kerry ate her evening meal alone and then sat in the lounge for a while reading magazines, with Coco at her feet, and finally took herself to bed. Tonight, again, the dog curled up on the rug, and when Louise arrived around midnight she said, 'Evening everybody. Is he a fixture?'

Coco growled without raising his head. 'Thank *you*,' said Louise. 'It's nice to be wanted.'

'Had a nice time?' asked Kerry.

'Lovely.' Louise began to explain that they had been to the next cove where they had spent the evening and had dinner in a small hotel called the Smugglers' Roost. 'By the way,' she said, 'both the Caradocs are bachelors. Adrian was engaged but it was broken off and no big deal apparently. David's never short of female company but they make the running, not him.'

'Where are you getting all this from?' Kerry asked, and Louise said smugly,

'I keep my ear to the ground. Actually I heard it where we ate. I asked the barmaid.'

'I should think that pleased Rob.'

'Not for me, for you.'

'Why for me?'

'Because,' said Louise, sounding like someone solving a problem, 'you need an affair. This is all very well and it's going to be a smashing holiday and we're all going to enjoy ourselves, but what you need while you're here is a dishy man around.' Rob was the apple of her eye but she still looked dreamy for a moment. 'And isn't he dishy? A fling with him would be something to remember.' She was quite shocked at herself. 'Well, that's what you need,' she insisted.

Kerry had had her flings. Although she had never been seriously involved, she had had a lively life until nearly four months ago. At the end of February while he sat at table for their evening meal, after a day like any other, without warning her father's heart had stopped. Since then nothing had seemed real. The suddenness, the unexpectedness had been traumatic. He was all the family she had, and she would miss him all her life, and afterwards nothing seemed to matter much.

She had been offered a good price for the driving school and the house that went with it and, after an initial reluctance, it had seemed sensible to sell. She didn't want to take it over, so she had taken the money, and although her friends were all finding her houses nearby she had an open mind. She didn't know yet where she would settle. Everywhere she went she considered. Penlyn certainly had its charms, and maybe Louise was right, a light-hearted affair with an attractive man would add to the fun of the holiday. But she couldn't see herself with either of the Caradocs. She hadn't met Adrian and it could take a lot longer than two weeks to get through to David. Besides, she didn't like David.

'No chance,' she said. 'Did you see his eye?' Louise giggled. 'And you should see what he did to me.'

She stretched out the arm with the fingerprint bruises while Louise made sympathetic noises. 'And now get some sleep,' said Kerry. 'We don't want Celia keeling over from exhaustion.'

'Not me,' said Louise chirpily, 'but I do hope Rob doesn't bump into any trees. You know he's blind as a bat without his glasses.'

'I'll lead him by the hand,' said Kerry as Louise began to get undressed and Louise gurgled,

'Don't you dare, he's spoken for.'

Robin and Louise made a good pair, but even if he had been free and available he wouldn't have quickened Kerry's pulse, although she still said, 'Lucky you,' because that was what Louise wanted to hear.

It was going to be a beautiful day for the start of the Flower Festival. They woke to sunshine and prettied up with particular care. A touch of make-up covered the bruises on Kerry's arm, and when they came dowstairs both girls were looking fetching and glowing with health.

By now all the guests knew them, and the first impression, that Louise was the more attractive, was changing. Louise was a very pretty girl, but it was Kerry who had the style. It wasn't clothes. They were both in simple dresses—Louise in pink, Kerry in yellow—but there was something about Kerry that made you look twice at her. Nice girls, both of them, but this morning when everyone was promising to go and see the play nobody was surprised that Kerry had the starring role.

'Shakespeare, is it?' grunted one man, who was plainly no fan, and Kerry pleaded,

'Please come, because it would be dreadful if nobody turned up. The garden's beautiful and we're really very good and it's really quite a funny play.'

The man's wife assured her they would be along one afternoon, and later as they walked around the town, passing an *As You Like It* poster in a window Louise said, 'You don't really think nobody will come and see us, do you? I mean, Mrs Caradoc's footing the bill at Wayside and everybody's being put up somewhere and it would be awful if we didn't make a profit for them.'

'Unless we play to a full garden,' said Kerry, 'we can always donate our board and lodging money.'

'Fair enough,' said Robin, 'although from the looks of

that place the Caradocs can afford to sponsor a bit of culture.'

'And with Erica and call-me-Penny on the committee,' said Kerry, 'I'm sure they have ways of getting the public in.'

This morning the show was in the streets, a carnival procession of floats and bands wound its way through the flower-decked town, with gaily dressed Morris dancers running along beside rattling collecting boxes. The carnival queen sat preening on her throne, surrounded by the three runners-up who had been created attendants as consolation prizes.

The floats all had baskets of flowers, small blooms that were tossed at intervals into the onlookers lining the pavements. Some of the girls and women laughed and scattered when a flurry of blossoms descended on the group where Kerry and Louise and Rob stood, but Rob caught a marigold and offered it to Louise.

'I'd think twice about takin' that, m'dear' said a chuckling matronly woman. 'It's said if a girl gets a flower she's expectin' within the twelve months, but if a man does it's going to be twins.'

Of course the Flower Festival would have fertility legends, all these traditional affairs did, and everyone around was laughing. Especially when a spry old fellow who looked as if he wouldn't see eighty again said, 'I'll risk it, lad,' and Louise yelped, 'Get rid, quick.'

There were stickers now pointing the way to Maen Bos and *As You Like It*, and two long banners stretched along the walls. Beside the gates a large board proclaimed 'Open at one-thirty. Show starts at two' and on the lawn of the standing rocks some WI Ladies were setting out a food and ice-cream and soft drinks stall.

It was a bustling scene. Folk were scuttling around and once again Penny Penrose greeted and directed them when they arrived on the front doorstep. Tickets were going like hot cakes, she reported gleefully, and of course more would be sold at the gate, and the little parlour had been set aside for them just along there.

It was a large parlour by Kerry's standards, although the Players nearly filled it, and there was a buffet in the kitchens and everyone was chattering and the depression that had never been far away since her father's death suddenly settled on her again.

She could control it. She had all along, but it made all the excitement seem empty and she slipped out of the room and the house, out again into the little spinney. It was quieter here. Not as silent as Thursday night, voices and music drifted across, but peaceful compared with the crush indoors, and she leaned against a tree, looking over the downs.

After this afternoon's performance she was free until Monday afternoon so there would be plenty of time for exploring, for walking. Mrs Hayle might let her take Coco. He was still missing his family, and heaven knew she was missing hers. Memories of her father overwhelmed her, and she brushed the back of her hand across her eyes. As Ruth said, she could act tears, but real sorrow left her with dry burning eyes and this heaviness like a lump of lead in her chest.

She made herself move, still walking through the trees, coming to the back of the hill of the arbour and farther along to the marquee. There was probably someone in there, probably Ruth, but she didn't want company and she skirted it and looked across at the grey stone studio and began to walk towards that.

She had taken a few steps before she checked herself. She would like him to watch this afternoon but if he didn't he'd surely see the play some time. And if he missed it altogether what did it matter? It would have been stupid to knock on that door and ask, 'Are you coming?' Yes or no, it didn't matter, and she might be wise to keep clear of David Caradoc. First impressions were often right and she had panicked when he had walked out of the shadows. Now she could stop to consider, but she could still easily imagine him as someone who would do her no good.

She turned back then and returned to the house. The others were having lunch but she was too nervous to eat more than a few mouthfuls of food before the perform-ance. It was a delicious summer buffet but Kerry was always a bundle of nerves before she stepped out on the stage. Then the spell began to work, and she became the character she was acting.

In the changing-tent her hands were so unsteady that she could hardly fix her head-dress, and the drop-pearls in the little paste diamond loops were trembling. 'Here, let me,' said Ruth, Kirbigripping it firmly in place in the chestnut curls that had been teased and curled into what looked like a great mane of hair.

The big eyes were theatrically made up now, gold-lidded, dark mascaraed lashes brushing her cheeks, and the high cheekbones were gleaming. She looked enchant-ing in her dark red dress and Ruth gave a little sigh. 'You look smashing; and so do you love.' Louise in a blue dress the colour of her eyes looked like Louise always did, very pretty. 'So do you all,' said Ruth, anxious to offend nobody, and Sandra and Jenny went on muttering their lines.

Tiers of seats had been set up at the end of the lawn, and those who hadn't got seats were sitting on the grass up to the roped-off area. The play started and for the second scene Kerry and Louise climbed up the little hill into the back of the round summer arbour, so that they could walk out of it down on to what was supposed to be the lawn before the Duke's palace.

There was a good-sized audience all looking expectantly at the girls and Louise as Celia began breathlessly, 'I pray thee, Rosalind, sweet my coz, be merry.'

Kerry's voice was stronger, very young and clear, and whether she was expressing her loneliness for the banished father or striving to be merry she was as convincing as though she were speaking her own words. At her first sight of Orlando she was briefly aware of Erica and David Caradoc in the seats behind him but that hardly registered as she fixed her eyes on Orlando, and asked, 'Is yonder the man?' with a catch in her voice.

By now she was Rosalind, witty and warm, carrying the sunlight with her. In real life Robin didn't turn her on at all, but as Orlando she fancied him like mad, and when she cried, 'That thou didst know how many fathom deep I am in love,' she meant it and the audience believed her. There was complete silence. Even the ice-cream eaters were spellbound.

For the wedding scene there was a quick change into girl's clothes again. She dragged the pins out of her hair that had been fastened close for a boy and it was back to the music and the song.

Then she turned to the Duke, her father, meek and demure. 'To you I give myself for I am yours.' And to Orlando the same words, but this time spoken with an undercurrent of passionate sexuality. Nobody doubted that Rosalind would deliver what she promised and that Orlando was a lucky man.

When the Players took their bow the audience applauded long and loud, especially when Robin kissed Kerry, although by now he was Rob again and the kiss meant nothing, and she looked to see if David Caradoc was clapping. He was, although not as energetically as Erica, who was giving them a standing ovation, and was in the changing-tent almost as soon as the girls were, still clapping.

'You were sensational,' cried Erica, 'It was——' She cast her eyes upwards for inspiration. 'It was *magnificent*. Do come out as soon as you can, there are *so* many people waiting to meet you.'

'Fame at last,' chirped Louise as Erica swept out of the tent again. But they were all pleased with themselves because it had gone well and when Kerry emerged, changed back into her yellow dress and her theatrical make-up toned down, she was greeted with smiles on all sides.

The festival committee seemed to be there in force, all agreeing that *As You Like It* should be a money-spinner, and that they had enjoyed the show immensely. 'An exceptionally high standard for amateurs,' Kerry heard one lady gushing to Gerald, who said coldly, 'We do our best, madam.' But most of the congratulations were not patronising. It was quite a triumph, and Kerry was saying, 'Thank you,' and 'That's very kind,' and she could see David Caradoc.

Everyone else seemed to be moving around, talking and laughing, but he was still. Being taller than most of them made him stand out, of course, and he was powerfully built. The breadth of his shoulders showed beneath a thin brown shirt and the sun glinted copper lights in his thick thatch of hair. Tawny, she thought, like a tiger, and not looking her way until Erica Caradoc caught her arm and said, 'Come and meet Adrian,' and trotted her to the outskirts of the crowd.

David said as they came up to him, 'I was wrong. You played your part superbly.'

'Thank you.' This was her moment and she savoured it, smiling smugly; and then a man who stood by said,

'She didn't play Rosalind at all, she *is* Rosalind,' and Erica said,

'This is Adrian.'

The resemblance to his mother was in the eyes and the mouth but he was fair-haired. A handsome young man, looking at Kerry like a star-struck boy. Only he was no boy and when he said, 'You are wonderful,' she blushed because the admiration was so personal that she felt almost shy. She had been acting a very sexy Rosalind just now but she had been acting, and she would have gone on to say how good the rest were and how lucky she was to be one of the Players, but David Caradoc said, 'So you can blush on cue too,' and his admiration was not so flattering. He was smiling at her more than with her, as though she amused him, and dammit, he did not amuse her.

She tried to ignore him and it shouldn't have been hard because Erica was taking her towards somebody else and Adrian was staying as close as her shadow, and she made sure that she never looked back in David's direction.

She didn't see him again, but all the time it was as though he was standing in the wings watching her act, and when after a few minutes Adrian asked, 'Have you seen the rose garden?' she said, 'I'd love to,' and breathed a sigh of relief as they walked away.

He said sympathetically, 'Does it tire you, giving a performance? It must be exhausting.'

'No,' she said. 'No. Something heavy, like Ibsen or Shakespeare's tragedies might, but this is a happy play, isn't it?'

'Then why were you sighing?'

She could hardly tell him, because being near your brother makes me hold my breath because I feel he is a dangerous man. Anyhow, that was rubbish, and she turned, smiling. 'That wasn't a sigh, that was a deep breath. It's this lovely sea air. Salt and roses are a heady combination.'

The rose garden was a garden in a garden, through a narrow iron gate in a high wall, sheltered from wind and trapping the sun. It contained a riot of roses from pure white to deepest red with herringbone-patterned paths made of old yellow bricks and stone seats set in arbours.

At the first seat Adrian pulled her gently down beside him. 'First question,' he said, 'you're not married?'

'No.'

'And no rings.' Her hands were bare but she laughed at that. 'So tell me all about yourself,' he said.

'There isn't much to tell.'

'I don't believe that.'

He could. There was nothing much she wanted to tell him. He looked across at her, his eyes were clear and steady and it was a sensitive face. 'Are you an artist?' she asked.

'A painter.'

'Your father was a sculptor?'

'That's right. You saw the stones?'

'They'd be hard to miss. I'd like to see your pictures.' He had an attractive smile when he said,

'I'd like to show them to you. Mind you,' he added, 'I'm not the artist David is. He's got a one-track mind when he's working. I'm more casual about the whole thing.'

Adrian would be easier altogether, she was sure, more understanding and less tough: and it was pleasant sitting here basking in his admiration because he was still looking at her as if she were the loveliest rose in the garden. David had eaten his words just now, about not seeing her as the sweetest rose, but no way could she imagine this look of wonder on his face.

'What do you do for a living?' Adrian was asking.

'I'm between jobs for the moment.

'Resting?'

'I'm not a professional actress. Although yes, I suppose I am resting right now, taking it easy for the next two weeks.'

'What are you doing for the rest of the day?'

'Maybe a walk over the downs.'

'We've got a tin-mine out there, the old Caradoc mine.' He never took his eyes off her. She was used to her share of male attention but nobody had ever carried on as though she dazzled them before, and it made her smile because it was absurd. 'You must show me some time,' she said. 'I'd like to see it.'

'There's not much to see. Just a ruin. It hasn't been worked this century.' He sighed. 'And I've got to get back to the Galleries.'

'The shop by the harbour?'

'That's right.'

'I went in yesterday.' She pulled a face that was a fair copy of the girl's expression. 'And met a better class of person.'

His smile was slightly lopsided. 'That would be Madeleine.'

'A friend of yours?'

The smile widened to a grin. 'It's not me she's after.' It was no business of Kerry's so she didn't follow that up, and when Adrian asked, 'Would you have dinner with me tonight?' she said,

'Thank you.'

She kept Coco on a lead until they were away from the road and, freed, he rushed around the downs, chasing goodness-knew-what but always coming back to her. The crowded little town and the lawns of Maen Bos with their capacity audience seemed very far away out here, where

Coco and mewing seagulls wheeling high in the sky seemed to be her only companions. There would be other walkers, of course, ones who had tired of the festival, but she was not meeting any.

Undulating hills and valleys stretched as far as she could see, and she could understand how easy it would be to get lost. She wasn't risking that, so she didn't stray far. She let Coco make the forays, calling him back if he looked like heading for the hills.

Heather and bracken grew thick, and when her skirt caught on a gorse bush she stooped to disentangle herself. There were stones underfoot here, big flat stones, broken and overgrown with weeds and grasses, but it had obviously been a track once. No, it was a road, quite a wide one. An old road, leading nowhere now or it wouldn't be so overgrown, but once it had led to the mine over the downs perhaps, and she could follow it and find her way back any time she chose.

'Follow the yellow brick road,' she carolled to Coco, who looked for the quarry and followed after her, tail swishing. It wasn't too difficult to trace the road; it went straight, and if you were looking there were occasional patches more or less visible.

Coco soon tired of chasing nothing and danced off after a Red Admiral butterfly, and Kerry plodded on.

She didn't have too far to go, about a quarter of a mile before she climbed a hill and down in a valley she could see the tall round chimney and grey stone buildings covered with ivy. The mine was a ruin, walls were crumbling and there were jagged gaps where windows had been, but she could imagine the chimney puffing and the sound of engines throbbing. And men, the tinners, trudging along the vanishing road.

Not for a hundred years, Adrian had said, but it was still the old Caradoc mine. She wondered what Caradocs had lived in Maen Bos in those days, generations back. She couldn't imagine Adrian as a Victorian mill owner, but David could have fitted the role.

He could be an arrogant brute, she was sure, haughty and overbearing, riding a splendid horse over the road she had just walked, dismounting down there and giving his orders.

The tin-mine had closed but Maen Bos still flourished; there was no sign of hard times there. Diamonds still flashed on Erica's hands and the furniture and paintings were obviously worth a fortune.

The very superior girl, whose name was Madeleine and who was not after Adrian, probably had her sights fixed on David. That was something of a joke from the way Adrian had smiled, but Kerry supposed they might make a not-too-ill-matched pair. From the little she had seen of Madeleine she could visualise her fitting as to the manner born into Maen Bos.

It had to be a good thing, she thought, that she was becoming curious again about what was going on around her. These last months she had tried to carry on as normally as possible, but she hadn't cared much about anything. Now she was standing here, wondering about a man and a woman she had met in the last couple of days. Neither was any concern of hers, but she still found them intriguing, and that was good. It meant that the change of scene and the pleasure of playing Rosalind were drawing her back again into the living world.

Coco was capering around below and she slid after him down the hill. There was a 'DANGER, KEEP OUT' notice, and a wire fence, but unless you were stupid enough to climb up on walls or pull down the boards across what was probably a shaft-head, there could surely be no harm in walking around. There wasn't much to see. Just the chimney and what were probably the engine rooms. Once there had been a row of buildings as well. Now they were hung thick with ivy, but when she came to the end she did a double-take because the last building had glass in the windows and a door. And there were tiles on the roof and a skylight.

Without stopping to think she tapped on the door and almost at once it opened. David Caradoc stood there, and he said what she would have said if she hadn't been struck dumb with surprise, 'I don't believe it. This is becoming ridiculous. What are you doing here?'

CHAPTER THREE

'CERTAINLY not following you,' snapped Kerry. She was hot and sticky, a little grimy and dishevelled. Usually that wouldn't have bothered her but she was annoyed at herself for knocking at his door looking as though she had crawled out of a ditch.

With anyone else she would have joked, 'We've got to stop meeting like this,' but now she said coolly, 'Actually I'm walking the dog,' although for the moment there was no sign of Coco.

'Not getting the atmosphere for another play?' He had a quiet voice but it would be carrying, she thought. A well controlled voice, just as he was a man of controlled energy, self-contained and sure of himself. She knew all this as she looked up at him now and heard herself babbling,

'I don't know a play down a tin-mine. The moors maybe. *Wuthering Heights*.'

'And I'm sure you'd make an excellent Cathy.' When he smiled it softened the lines of his face and she said,

'Maybe Mrs Caradoc will let us turn the lawns into the Yorkshire moors next year.'

'She might indeed.'

'I hear she was an actress.'

'She is an actress. All the world's a stage for Erica.' He sounded amused.

'Well, I think she's smashing, and we're all so pleased she invited us down and we're hoping the sun keeps shining.'

'So am I,' he said, 'or she's turning the house into the Forest of Arden.'

Indoors if wet, it had said on the posters, and she
grinned because she could see the funny side of that. It
looked as though Erica Caradoc had the say-so on what
happened in Maen Bos but David Caradoc might
consider the Players acting up and down the stairs, and
traipsing along the gallery, as an invasion of privacy.

'Remember it's all in a good cause,' she said and he
shook his head ruefully.

'The times I've heard that.' And then they were both
smiling.

Coco came racing up, panting so that it looked more
than ever as though he was grinning. 'This is my dog,' she
said, and wondered if the Hayles might let her adopt him.
They might if she stayed down here, and that would be
somebody to talk to in the empty hours. 'He's a hunting
dog right now,' she said. 'He's been on the trail ever since
we got on to the downs.'

'Rabbits?'

'I think it's birds and butterflies. He does most of his
rushing about with his nose in the air, so he's more likely
to fall over a rabbit than catch one.'

'I should keep him away from here. The entrance
shafts are filled in but a dog might squirm through
somewhere and not get out too easily.'

'And the old mine's still down there?' That was a silly
question. Of course it was. In miles of dark winding
passages, full of mud and debris. She put out a hand for
Coco. 'We should be getting home. What is this place?'
The end building with windows and roof.

'A workroom,' he said, 'where I can usually rely on not
being disturbed.'

He said it smiling but he wasn't asking her in and she
could hardly call again after that, so she said, 'We've got
to stop meeting like this,' and gave him her most flashing
smile, and went back to the old road with the sun still
shining and the wind blowing through her hair.

As she walked she was aware of a lightness in her step and smiled again at the idea of Erica Caradoc's good causes, and David's laughter. There had been a lot of talk and sympathy in her life of late. But this brief encounter had seemed to blow away the cobwebs as though the shadows were beginning to lift.

It was after six when Kerry and Coco got back to Wayside. She had explained earlier to Mrs Hayle that she would not be in for the evening meal, and up in the bedroom Louise was waiting, with a large bouquet of dark red roses lying in the washbasin in the corner.

They caught Kerry's eye as soon as she walked into the room. Roses from Rob. 'Why don't you put them in a vase?' she asked.

'It isn't from Rob, said Louise. 'They're not mine. They're yours. There's the card.'

A little white envelope was on the dressing-table and Kerry had no doubt that Louise had opened it the moment she was alone. On the outside it read, 'Kerry Holland, Wayside Guest House,' and the card inside was handwritten, 'Red roses for Rosalind, Adrian Caradoc.'

Although the writing was clear enough, she read 'David' for a split second, and for another couple of seconds she could hardly remember Adrian's face.

'Well, how about that?' trilled Louise, reading the card with a very good show of this being the first time. 'From *Adrian* Caradoc. Now I never saw Adrian but I was told you'd gone off with him. And you're not in for dinner tonight, so isn't that just what your Auntie Lou ordered? What's he like?'

'Handsome,' said Kerry.

'As good-looking as his brother?'

'Different. But you will see him because he's calling for me at seven.'

'Oh, well,' said Louise, trying to sound casual, 'I might just happen to be around. Mrs Hayle left you a vase.'

The vase was big and bulbous, pink cabbage roses on matt black, and the two dozen long-stemmed red roses made an impressive sight. Kerry put them on the window ledge and Louise said, 'I do think giving a girl flowers is so romantic,' and Kerry said,

'Well, Rob gave you a marigold this morning,' and Louise shrieked,

'No, he didn't, I swear I never touched it. Maybe we could make up a foursome some time. Not tonight of course, this being your first date, but later on, maybe.'

'If I'm asked again,' said Kerry, and Louise went down to join Rob for dinner and Kerry went to the wardrobe to choose a dress.

Adrian Caradoc seemed a promising companion for an evening out on the town: presentable, intelligent and anxious to please. And even this nonsense about being star-struck with her Rosalind was not a bad thing. She had never been a girl for serious commitments; this had to be just a bit of play-acting, and she was good at that.

She wore a bright pink dress, sleeveless and low-backed, and she added sparkle with a pair of gold sandals, and a gold snake bracelet that she had yearned over in a jeweller's window and that was her father's last Christmas gift to her.

'Oh, *yes*,' said Louise, coming back into the bedroom as Kerry sprayed perfume on pulse points, 'you look fantastic.'

'Thank you.' She was feeling good, her smooth tanned skin glowed and her eyes danced. A date with a man whose first words to her had been 'You are wonderful' had to be an ego-boost.

'I'm having my coffee in the lounge,' said Louise, who must have bolted her dinner. 'Don't you think you should be coming down, it's nearly seven?'

Kerry laughed. 'I wouldn't dream of slipping out without giving you a chance of seeing Adrian,' and

Louise giggled, unrepentant.

'I'm interested, aren't I? I thought David was sensational; I want to see why you picked Adrian.'

'Because Adrian was the one who asked me,' said Kerry.

'Suppose David had?' Louise had been very struck with David Caradoc.

'He won't,' said Kerry.

'You could always ask him,' Louise suggested, and Kerry laughed again.

'I'm only here for a fortnight, I'll take the one who sent the roses.' She didn't say 'David would turn me down. He only does what *he* wants to do and he doesn't want an affair with me.' And she most assuredly did not wish to get involved with him. Her instincts told her he could be too much for her in every way and that playing safe with Adrian would be a surer way of enjoying her holiday.

Adrian was punctual. On the dot of seven he walked into the foyer and Kerry came out of the lounge with Louise hovering behind her. 'Not bad at all,' murmured Louise, 'but if I were you I'd still ask David.'

'Hello,' said Kerry. She gripped Louise's arm and drew her forward. 'And this is my friend Louise who was Celia, you remember?'

'Yes, of course,' said Adrian. 'How do you do?'

'She's dying to meet you,' said Kerry, 'because you make up the set. You are the last of the Caradocs?'

'I suppose I am.' He smiled at Louise, who gave him a perky grin back.

'All right?' said Kerry.

'Yes,' said Louise. 'Have a good time, then.'

'You too,' said Kerry, and now Louise would go back to Rob and describe Adrian Caradoc for him. He was a good-looking young man, fair hair waving back from a high brow, well dressed and well spoken. Louise would probably be quite enthusiastic about Adrian and afterwards perhaps she would shut up about David.

'The roses were lovely,' said Kerry as they walked out into the car park. 'Did you pick them from the garden?'

'No, I got them from the shop next to the gallery.' She had known from the wrapping that they were shop flowers, but she smiled at the small joke and said,

'They're beautiful, thank you.'

'I didn't know she was Celia,' said Adrian. 'I didn't see Celia. I didn't see anyone but Rosalind.'

'It must have been a very odd *As You Like It* you were watching.'

'It was an *As You Like It* I shall always remember.' He stopped and looked admiringly at her, and she smiled because she didn't want him getting serious. She wanted a light-hearted evening out, and she moved on a few steps and asked, 'Do we walk or ride?'

'We take the car.'

'Yours or mine? That's mine, with the advert on it.' She pointed to her yellow car with its scarlet slogan, explaining, 'I worked in the office of a driving-school. I got a petrol allowance for the advert; I must get it resprayed.'

She had sold the dual-control car with the rest but somehow she couldn't get herself to wipe out the name on this car; it was as if when she did, her last link with that part of her life would snap.

'You're not working there now?' His car was a gleaming Nissan Silvia Turbo. He opened the door and she slid into the passenger seat. She had told him she was between jobs and she said, 'It closed down.' She didn't want to talk about her father, nor about herself, and she got him talking about himself easily enough.

He had had an easy life by any standards. Caradocs had built Maen Bos nearly two hundred years ago and lived there ever since. The name meant stone dwelling, and it must always have been as solid and secure as a rock because all along the Caradocs had prospered. Adrian had gone through public school and art school and now he ran the Galleries down by the harbour and painted his pictures.

She kept him talking as they took the winding coastal road and when he said, 'What about you? Tell me about your family,' she said lightly,

'I have none, but I'm hoping to adopt a dog.' Then she told him about Coco who was such a good listener and that she had walked over the downs with the dog this afternoon and found the old road.

'We followed it to the mine,' she said. 'How long since it closed?'

'Fourteen, fifteen years.'

She hadn't expected that. 'But didn't you say not this century?'

'It hasn't been worked for a hundred years, but my father had some idea of making it a tourist attraction. There was quite a lot of work done before he decided it wasn't practical and had it closed down again.'

She was going to say, 'I saw David,' but that was when they turned to take a precipitously steep and twisting road down towards the sea, and Adrian said, 'This is one of the Caradoc beaches.'

'Your own beaches?' She hadn't thought anyone owned the sands, but he said,

'A fair stretch. The properties are leased. They do a good meal at the hotel.'

Louise would be fascinated to hear that Adrian Caradoc was not only handsome but rich. The little harbour was a miniature Penlyn, boats drawn up on the sand, holiday-makers, one shop and a row of white-painted cottages with a few more clinging to the hillside. The hotel was built right on the rocks and the windows of the dining-room looked over the sea.

They were greeted like VIPs. Well, a Caradoc would

be a VIP down here, but it was the first time Kerry had been shown to her table with quite such smiling affability. Talk about star treatment, she thought, and the whole thing was like a scene in a play. From the setting to the handsome young man who was hardly touching the lobster thermidor that she was wolfing down. She didn't get meals like this every day even if he did, and the sea air was making her ravenous.

'Do you believe in love at first sight?' he said in low intense tones, looking at her as if she were all the nourishment he needed, and she had to swallow what she was chewing before she could say,

'Only on stage.' And then it faded as soon as the play ended.

'I do after this afternoon.' The dining-room was full, so there was chatter from other tables to drown their conversation as they sat at this window a little removed from the rest. 'Since I saw you as Rosalind,' he said, 'it was like a bolt from the blue.'

The compliment made her smile, and he reached to take the hand that wasn't holding a fork, and asked, 'Can I call you Rosalind?'

She shrugged. 'You can call me anything you like as long as you don't always expect me to answer to it.'

It *was* make-believe, pure escapism; and the food was delicious and she was prepared to sing for her supper playing Rosalind for him, so for the rest of the meal she turned in a performance of gaiety and charm. Which wasn't hard because both were natural to her. She made him smile and she saw the desire that kindled in his eyes and she knew she could handle that and she was enjoying herself.

Afterwards they walked along the fringe of the beach. By now the moon was up and the tide was coming in and she carried her sandals and splashed through the white foam, cold waves lapping her ankles, the sand firm and

gritty between her toes. Adrian walked beside her, and
every so often a wave reached him, breaking over his
shoes. They were suede and looked expensive, but when
she said, 'You're ruining your shoes,' he gestured
dismissively and she joked, 'That's wealth, knowing
where your next pair of good shoes are coming from.'

'Don't you?'

'Yes, but I don't buy gold kid sandals every day,' and
she swung them high above the splashing spray. They
were hand-made and had been an extravagance last
summer. This year she had bought hardly anything,
mostly because she had no heart for buying.

'My feet aren't as pretty as yours,' he said.

'I should hope not.'

'Pretty hands, pretty feet.'

'Thank you,' she said gaily. 'I've no complaints, they
all seem to work reasonably well.'

He was pretty, she thought, although he moved as if
there was an athletic body under that beautifully cut
light-weight suit. His skin was lightly tanned, as
naturally pale as his mother's, and he had her chiselled
features, her dark eyes.

He looks like the artist, she thought, the poet, the
dreamer. David could be anything that was tough and
powerful. Over the meal Adrian had held her hand, and
his were the kind of hands you would expect an artist to
have, slim and long-fingered. Very nice hands. The only
touch she had had from David was a no-holds-barred
scrap, and it had been nearly dark and she hadn't looked
at his hands. And then with clay on them when Erica
trooped the Players into the studio. And when he stood
talking to her by the mine. But she knew they were strong
and capable. David could probably build a house that
would stand as long as Maen Bos, she thought absurdly,
and she wondered how it would be to have him caress her
and she couldn't even begin to imagine. That was strange

because she had a vivid imagination, but no way could she envisage David Caradoc's tender touch.

'Don't you think so?' said Adrian. She was paddling along, thinking her thoughts, and she had no idea what he had been talking about so she said hastily,

'Oh, yes.'

But before she could discover what she was agreeing with they had reached the end of the little stretch of sand. They had already turned once where the cliffs rose and retraced their vanished steps at the water's edge. But when she turned this time Adrian stepped into the sea and grabbed her in his arms, clutching her to him, and said in a choked voice, 'God, how I want you! I'm mad about you.' She burst out laughing. The cold water was up to their knees and, in spite of the warmth of the evening, cool enough, she would have thought, to dampen anyone's ardour, and he said raggedly, 'See what you do to me. With the moonlight on your hair you're so beautiful you dazzle me.'

She linked an arm in his arm and walked him out of the sea and told him, 'I don't believe in love at first sight, nor in lovemaking at first meeting. Especially not on the rocks at the height of the tourist season.'

There were other strollers on the beach and they were just under the windows of the hotel, spotlit in an arc of light. Adrian would hardly have been likely to try for more than a kiss, but he began to apologise. 'I'm sorry, I lost my head.' She sat down on a rock to mop her feet with a tissue and slip on her sandals before stepping on to the stony shingle.

'You've done for your shoes now,' she said.

'Have I done for myself?' He sounded quite desperate. 'I'd hate to think I'd spoiled things.'

'How?' All he had done was hold her.

'Do you like me?'

'Of course. Or I wouldn't be here.'

'I'm in love with you.' He sat on the shingle beside her rock. 'I've been waiting for you all my life.'

She had come across that line before, but only in books and plays, and this was play-acting, all these dramatics, and if it was going on she would have to make her role clear. It would be fun to go around with Adrian while she was down here, but she didn't want a heavy physical relationship. As she finished buckling the second sandal she said, 'I've enjoyed tonight and I do *like* you very much.' She laid light emphasis on the word. 'But I should say any chance of our becoming lovers in the next two weeks are highly remote.'

'It doesn't matter,' he was eager to reassure her. 'We can be friends, we can get to know each other, although I feel already that I know everything about you. You're Rosalind, what more is there to know?'

'So I am,' she said, 'for the next two weeks.'

They said good night in Wayside car park and she couldn't object to what was an undemanding kiss. Cool lips brushed her cheek and fastened for a moment on her mouth, and arms enveloped her briefly. Then he drew back and they were smiling into each other's eyes.

'Till tomorrow,' he said.

'I'll be along.' She stood with folded arms, watching the car draw out and away, and turned to meet Louise and Coco coming across to her.

'Well?' said Louise. 'Is he as nice as he looks?'

'Yes, he is.'

'Well, tell me about it.' Louise kept in step with her and Coco followed a couple of stairs behind so that when Kerry reached her bedroom and looked at them they both appeared to be waiting for an account of her evening.

She almost said, 'We had a meal and we talked and I'm seeing him tomorrow,' but that would have been like disappointing a child over a bedtime story, Louise wanted to hear much more than that. So instead she sat on the bed and started with the cove that belonged to the Caradocs. She acted out their welcome at the hotel, described the food, and the wine which had been a special bottle produced with reverence by the head waiter. And finally the stroll along the beach in the moonlight, and how Adrian had taken her in his arms and said he was mad about her and that her beauty dazzled him.

Louise, who had been listening enthralled, suddenly suspected that Kerry was exaggerating. 'He fell for my Rosalind,' said Kerry. 'I know that sounds crazy, but he's a fan, and he really did say that I dazzled him.'

Louise thought about that, then said, 'Well, I suppose you are beautiful. Sometimes you are when you're acting. You're a knockout all the time, of course, but you can look sensational when you're acting.'

That was the aura of beauty that Kerry could produce when she was deep into a part, and now she wrinkled her nose. 'It's all a trick, all done with mirrors. But he's starstruck for me and it's flattering. It makes me feel like a star.'

'Just what you needed.' Louise was all in favour. 'So enjoy it.'

With no harm done and no danger of pain. The only man who had ever hurt Kerry had been her father. His death, with its sudden withdrawal of love and support, had seemed like a betrayal. No one could take a father's place, but it would be a long time before she risked letting anyone again get close enough to matter much.

She ran fingers through her hair, ruffling it loose, and took off her sandals. 'I shall sleep tonight,' she said, as she drew down the snake bracelet that encircled her upper arm and winced slightly at its pressure on the fading bruises. Adrian's kiss had skimmed the surface, but that was a touch that had gone deep.

'I'm having a meal at the house tomorrow evening,' she said, and wondered if David would be there . . .

There was no performance of *As You Like It* on Sunday, so Kerry spent most of the next day swimming and sunbathing. The bay was full of boats and swimmers and surfers while the beach was crowded with sun-worshippers, well oiled and browning comfortably. Louise and Robin and Kerry met several other Players and they settled themselves on a smooth shelf of rock with a small cave, well above the water-line of a summer sea.

When the storms came anyone standing there would risk being snatched away, but today it was lovely with the shelter of the cave for those who weren't wanting a sun tan and room for those who were to stretch out.

In a white bikini, and covered with suntan oil, Kerry was revelling in the sunshine, drowsing the hours away. Even when she swam it was a lazy day. She was a good swimmer and she was putting no effort into it, floating and drifting, then climbing back up the rocks to towel herself dry and slosh on more oil.

They bought fruit and Cornish pasties, sandwiches, cider and cans of Coke from takeaways on the harbour, and picknicked and made plans for when they were not performing the plays: fishing trips, visits to beauty spots. If the weather continued like this it was going to be a fantastic holiday.

'And that house,' said Jenny, 'you should see our bedroom. We've got a four-poster with hanging curtains.' She was a pale girl with light ginger hair who freckled easily and was sitting in the shadows. 'We're really living it up, aren't we, Griff?'

'The Caradocs must be loaded. You should have seen the glasses we were drinking wine out of last night,' said Griff, pouring cider into paper cups.

'If only I were single,' Jenny sighed theatrically, 'I'd

make a pitch for one of them. They're neither of them married.'

'Have you seen much of them?' Kerry was lying on her back, eyes shut against the glare.

'Not after yesterday afternoon,' said Jenny, 'but they live there, don't they?'

'Kerry was out with Adrian last night.' Louise liked passing on gossip almost as much as she enjoyed hearing it. Kerry had never told her anything in confidence and she wasn't sure whether she would trust Louise with a secret. '*And* he sent her a great bunch of red roses,' said Louise.

That started the tongues wagging. They teased her about that, and she lay, with her eyes still closed, smiling at them. 'You'll be the young Mrs Caradoc maybe next year,' gurgled Jenny, 'and then you can invite us all down again for the Festival. And please can we have the four-poster bed?'

'Red roses do not make a wedding ring,' Kerry intoned. 'This is just a holiday romance and don't any of you forget it.'

'He said——' Louise began and Kerry finished,

'And any more from you and it's the last time I let you read the messages on my roses.'

What with the cider and the sun and the murmuring lullaby of voices and lapping water she dozed off until William came dripping wet out of the sea and shook himself like a dog all over her. Then she asked, 'What time is it?'

When somebody told her she yawned, and sighed because she had promised to be at the Galleries by six and now she would have to rush up to Wayside to bath and change and then get back down here. Sitting up, she could see that nobody else seemed to have gone yet. The beach and the street were still crowded and she would have to work her way through the throng and she didn't feel that energetic.

She reached for her pink and white striped cotton beach-bag and took out a white cheesecloth dress and slipped on flatties. 'I'm away,' she declared, pulling the dress over her head.

'She has a date,' Louise announced.

'With Adrian Caradoc?' they all chorused and Kerry laughed and went off along the rock ledge towards the town, hearing Louise telling them,

'That's who she's seeing *and* he said he was mad about her.'

There was no sign of Madeleine in the Galleries this afternoon. A middle-aged man, burly and bearded, seemed to be in charge. As she looked around for Adrian the man said, 'You're Rosalind?'

'At times,' she said.

'I hear you're good.'

'That's kind of somebody.'

'Adrian's up in the studio.' A white iron staircase spiralled upwards and she thanked him and began to climb it and he said, 'Hope it keeps fine for you. Last year's Flower Festival ended in three days of force-eight gales.'

'That should put a new slant on the Forest of Arden,' she called back down the stairs and she stepped through the door at the top into a working studio the width of the upper floor, with easels and paintings—some half finished, some stacked against the wall. Beyond an archway was another room, where Adrian was sitting at a Queen Anne desk by the window, speaking on the telephone.

He had heard her and he was smiling as she came through the archway. 'I won't be a minute. Do sit down.'

She was covered in sand and oil, and she looked apprehensively at sofas and chairs which all appeared to be upholstered in material that was probably irreplaceable. It was a beautiful room, furnished like Maen Bos with antiques, and with two jewel-bright Moroccan rugs on the polished floor. Downstairs the Galleries sold old and new paintings, from long-dead artists and work where the paint was hardly dry, but this room was a period piece.

She did sit down, keeping gleaming bare legs and arms away from the brocade, and after a few more words Adrian said goodbye to whoever he was talking to and put down the phone and came across to her. 'You're early,' he said. 'That's nice.'

'No, I'm late. I overslept on the beach and I looked in to say I'm going back now to get tidied up and ask if you could collect me from Wayside.'

'I could but why don't you just relax for another half-hour and have a coffee and then I'll take you to my home. There'll be a bathroom there you can use.'

She had a modicum of make-up in her beach-bag, and a coffee would be welcome, and she would enjoy looking around the galleries much more than rushing up the hillside to Wayside. 'That sounds a very good idea,' she said gratefully.

She was still sitting in her chair, sprawling slightly but with a natural grace. A window drape of faded pink and lilac made a misty background to her youthful vibrancy, and Adrian said, 'I wish I were a portrait painter so that I could paint you there, like that.'

'What do you paint?'

He showed her a picture on an easel, an abstract of vistas all light and space, and she admired it and she did like it. It would have been easy to live with, there was nothing about it to trouble anyone.

She was given a cup of Cappuccino coffee and she wandered around, staring her fill at all the exhibits, then the doors closed and Adrian came looking for her. 'Good

night, Rosalind,' said the bearded man whose name was
Adam and who was a potter, and she began to say 'Kerry'
then changed it to 'Good night,' because while she was
down here why not answer to the name she was playing?
What actress didn't want to be Rosalind?

They made slow progress through the narrow roads of
the town, which were packed solid now with departing
cars. Surely it would have been easier, Kerry thought, for
Adrian to have walked down in the morning, but he said,
'I need transport for fetching and carrying,' and she
answered,

'I'm not grumbling, it's a lovely car to ride in.'

She relaxed into the cushioning leather seat and they
climbed the hill slowly enough for her to look in shop
windows, coming to a standstill by an estate agent's. She
had read notices in here earlier, walking down to the
harbour, and now she asked, 'Where's Glenoral
Terrace?'

'Up there.' He pointed to the left and high. 'Why?'

'There's a cottage for sale.'

'You're interested?' He began to smile.

'I've just sold my house, so wherever I go I look in
estate agents' windows.'

Adrian's smile widened with delight. 'But that would
be *marvellous*,' and he sounded just like his mother. 'If
that isn't fate I don't know what is. You're looking for
somewhere to live and you've come to the very place.'

She wished she had thought before she spoke because
now she might be pressured, and even if an ideal house
were found for her here there would be problems.
Earning a living of course, and Adrian. If she took up
residence in Penlyn he wouldn't expect their relationship
to stay platonic. She could keep it cool for a fortnight, but
much longer and she would need a good reason for
holding him at arm's length.

His pride would be hurt if she said, 'You're very

attractive but I don't want anybody getting too close just now. So friendship is in but sex is out. Nothing personal.' But of couse he would take it personally, so at the end of the run of *As You Like It* she would probably be leaving with the others.

The car edged upwards and she said, 'I'm not deciding anything in a hurry,' and she asked him about one of the pictures she had seen in the Galleries, an old oil painting of a woman who looked bad-tempered, and listening to Adrian's account of the life of the artist passed the time until they turned into the road that led to Maen Bos.

As Kerry got out of the car in the courtyard at the back of the house the housekeeper came over. Mrs Bunbury had a smooth round face and smooth dark hair parted in the middle and drawn back, and she reminded Kerry of Mrs Bun the baker's wife from a pack of Happy Family cards. 'Mr Letheridge is waiting to see you, Mr Adrian,' she said. 'In the study.'

'It's about an exhibition,' Adrian explained to Kerry, and to Mrs Bunbury, 'Would you take Miss Holland to a bathroom? She's come straight from the beach and she wants a shower.'

'Certainly,' said Mrs Bunbury. There were at least four guests, not to mention the family, but she seemed to have no doubts about a vacant bathroom being available.

'I'll see you downstairs as soon as you're through,' said Adrian, and Kerry went with the housekeeper into the house, along a flag-stoned passage and up a narrow flight of stairs, while Mrs Bunbury chatted on about the lovely weather and hoped Kerry was enjoying her stay.

'Here we are, miss.' She opened a bedroom door then the door of a connecting bathroom. 'I think you'll find everything in here you need.'

I should think so too, thought Kerry. Soaps and bath lotions and fluffy white towels. It was a big room for a bathroom, with cupboards and panelled walls, and ornate Victorian bath, taps and washbasin and loo. A shower cabinet struck a modern note and no doubt the plumbing had been up-dated, but it was the kind of bathroom into which you could take a good book, run a scented bath and spend a leisurely evening.

It seemed a shame just to take a shower but she hadn't time for any more, and the bedroom was quite something too. Frilled and feminine with an old engraved silver vanity set on the white and gold dressing-table. There was no sign of occupation, it could have been a room in a glossy magazine, and she picked up the hand mirror and wondered how many faces had been reflected in that down the years.

Not many like her. They would all be elegant ladies and she looked like a gipsy with her shiny skin and her sea-bedraggled hair, and she stepped out of her shoes and went back into the bathroom, and took off her bikini and dress.

There was so much oil on her that she had to lather and rub vigorously to shift it, and then she washed her hair and stood with her head thrown back letting the water stream down over her upturned face. She would have to dry her hair and set it somehow and put on some make-up and go down and be sociable, but for the moment she felt as if all her tensions and troubles were gurgling away down the plughole.

You really felt safe in a bathroom like this. They didn't build them this way any more, so opulent and solid. She wondered if the other bathrooms in Maen Bos were all Victorian, she must ask the Players who were staying there if they knew. Louise would be fascinated to hear about the bath with the delicate trace of Willow pattern and four huge bronze clawed feet.

She heard the door open and close and froze, and then David Caradoc said, 'You're back early.' Water filled her gaping mouth so that she could only gurgle. Who did he think was in here? She had locked the door, so how the hell had he opened it, and what was Mrs Bunbury playing at, putting her into a bathroom which David Caradoc shared with somebody who had the room with the frills which sure as God made little apples was not his bedroom?

She didn't turn off the shower, it was as if the water was some form of cover for her, and she heard more taps go on and she had to stop him stripping for a bath, but it was the hardest thing in the world to open the shower door and put her head out. And if she just called he might open the door. He had to be on pretty intimate terms with whoever he thought was showering, he might think it was a joke if she yelled, 'Get out.'

She eased the door back a fraction and squinted through, and he was at the washbowl, his back to her, and she shut it again and leaned against the tiled wall, the shower still running, clutching a face cloth which could only provide a ridiculous cover.

He wasn't stripping off, he was stripped. All but a towel knotted at the waist and that didn't look too secure, and she couldn't think what she could do, except stay in here until he got out, keep the water running and pretend she couldn't hear. At least he wasted no time washing, shaving, because quite soon it was quiet and when she peered out again the bathroom was empty.

There was a door she hadn't noticed, in the panelling and over-shadowed by a floor-to-ceiling linen cupboard. It was shut but it must lead to another bedroom, and she grabbed a towel and her clothes. She had left her shoes and beach-bag beside the dressing-table but she wasn't hanging around. She rubbed herself comparatively dry as fast as possible, although her hair was still dripping, slipped into shoes and dress and shot out of the room.

She didn't know whether she was angry or whether it was funny. she was shaking with something that could have been laughter. Mrs Bunbury must have presumed she would lock both doors, only she hadn't *seen* both doors, and David Caradoc must be in the habit of wandering in through an unlocked door wearing next to nothing at all.

Kerry had to get on something under this cheesecloth dress, and when she saw Ruth and Gerald come out of a door at the end of the long corridor she called 'Hey.'

They rounded the corner then and she hurried after them but when she reached the corner herself they were out of sight and she turned back.

This last room must be theirs, and she stepped inside to put on her bikini. Ruth and Gerald's belongings were all round, including Ruth's hair-dryer on the bedside table, and Kerry helped herself to a little make-up. Ruth wouldn't mind and the moisturiser in her own bag might not be enough when the story came out of how she had been trapped in the shower.

She might manage to laugh it off or she might blush scarlet. She was taking no chances and she patted a liberal layer of Ruth's foundation cream on her cheeks. She had a mascara wand and lipstick with her and she used them both and dried her hair, pushing it into deep waves and fastening it back with a couple of Ruth's Kirbigrips.

She took her time because she was reluctant to go downstairs and face them all. Perhaps David Caradoc had realised that the girl in the shower was somebody else and that was why he had got out fairly quickly. She couldn't see him spreading the tale but if they did hear about it what was Kerry going to say? 'I'd have spoken up if you'd had any clothes on.' That would have them rolling the in the aisles.

At first she had been speechless with shock, and then she had felt so vulnerable being naked, even behind the opaque glass of the doors. He had looked powerful, the broad shoulders and the smooth strength of muscles rippling the skin. There was a bad scar across his right shoulder, a long white jagged line from shoulder blade to spine. The towel was loosely fastened at the waist and the legs were lean and long. Naked he had been more overpowering than ever. She could not have stood up to him, so she had shut eyes and ears and gone on cowering in the cabinet.

Well, she was out now, and she wished she had woken earlier on the beach and had something smarter than a sloppy cheesecloth dress to wear. From the glimpse she had caught of Ruth and Gerald they were done up to the nines, Gerald in a dark grey suit, Ruth in her little black chiffon number that she always wore with her real pearls.

Kerry's dress had a drawstring neckline and she pulled out the string and eased the dress down over her shoulders. The bikini was strapless and her shoulders were brown and smooth and maybe the effect wasn't bad. It was still a cheap dress but who cared? Only she would have liked to look as good as any of them tonight, and she wondered if it was Madeleine who slept in the room with the communicating doors, and if she would be there.

Well, Adrian would think Kerry was fetching because Adrian was stage-struck with Rosalind and she remembered what Louise had said, 'You can look sensational when you're acting.' She could pretend that this was a beautiful dress, and that the bikini was silk against her skin. She could think herself beautiful, and she stood for a moment in Ruth and Gerald's bedroom, hands pressed together imagining she was in the wings of a theatre about to step on stage, waiting for the flow of adrenalin that would carry her into the part she was to play.

She found her way to the minstrels' gallery and the sound of voices and laughter rose from the drawing-room below. There must be quite a gathering in there but the wide curved staircase and the hall were empty and she took a deep breath, held her head high and swanned down, trailing one hand along the dark polished oak bannister, waving the other in gracious greeting.

She enjoyed that. It was fun, making a grand entrance. If the weather should break, the staircase and hall and gallery would be an exciting theatre. She almost hoped it would rain, just for one performance.

The drawing-room door was wide open and David Caradoc stood just inside. As she met his ironic glance she thought he might have watched her, waving to nobody as she came downstairs. And she looked hastily away because it was bad enough wondering if he knew she had been in the shower without worrying about just making a fool of herself walking down the staircase.

'Rosalind,' said Adrian, and as Kerry stepped forward David clapped, a couple of slow handbeats, and somebody else took it up so that there was a little burst of applause. It was friendly, there were smiles, but it made her hold her head even higher because she knew that David Caradoc was sending her up, even if nobody else in the room realised that.

She should have dressed for dinner. As she walked into the drawing-room she saw Penny Penrose, wearing something that glittered, and Erica in another of her flowing robes. This one was in purple and cerise and she wore heavy antique earrings and a collar of amethysts and seed pearls. This wasn't just an evening meal, this was a full-scale dinner-party. 'Think silk,' Kerry exhorted herself, reaching Adrian and wishing she were somewhere else.

Erica could hardly have been more welcoming. She held out both hands as if Kerry were the guest she had been waiting for, although she probably did that to everybody, Kerry thought, and she said archly, 'Adrian has been telling me how impressed he was with your Rosalind.'

'Thank you,' Kerry murmured, and Erica gushed on.

'Everyone was impressed, of course, we all know the play is going to be a *great* success, but when Adrian told me last night how enchanting he thought you were do you know what I thought?' Kerry shook her head and everyone around listened, although Erica was talking behind tapering fingers as if this were a secret between herself and Kerry. 'I remembered that I met my husband for the first time after he had seen me playing Beatrice. He always said he fell in love with me then.' Although she might be recalling something that actually happened she still sounded like an actress speaking her lines, when she declared throbbingly, 'Ours was a marriage of twin souls, we were all in all to each other, so I think that this is very romantic and thrilling.'

She looked at Adrian, and her smile included them both and Kerry felt she might well say, 'Bless you, my children,' but what she did say was, 'You remind me of myself at your age, we are very alike.'

Erica Caradoc was a beautiful woman in a totally different mould from Kerry. It was the look of vitality, aliveness, that made Kerry stand out in a crowd, but Erica had perfect features. They were both tallish and both had strong hair waving back, but that was the only physical resemblance. They were both actresses, but Kerry felt that Erica existed on another plane from real life as she herself knew it.

'You remind me of myself, we are very alike,' was a compliment, but the only honest answer would have been, 'No we are not.' Only of course Kerry said, 'Well, thank you,' and Adrian nodded agreement and several people around murmured 'Yes.'

Erica and Adrian were both smiling at Kerry, so was half the room at the little tableau of Erica holding her hand and Adrian's arm around her shoulder, and David—some malicious force kept drawing Kerry's gaze towards David—looked like a cynical observer watching a situation that must not be allowed to get out of hand.

CHAPTER FOUR

THE dining-room had dark red walls, pictures in dark gold frames, and a crystal chandelier hanging over a table that could have seated twenty. There were a dozen around it tonight, with Erica one end and David the other. Madeleine was on David's right, and Kerry—to her acute discomfort—found herself seated on his left.

Next to Adrian, true, but she would much rather have been up the other end. Even better, out of the house altogether. Adrian really should have mentioned the kind of meal she was being invited to. And she was wishing now that she hadn't pulled the drawstring out of her dress because it kept slipping too far down over her shoulders and needing hitching up again if she wasn't to present a very raffish picture.

Madeleine looked quite at home. In the Galleries she was tight-lipped, as if nobody she could see was of much interest to her, but now she was smiling. Mostly at David, although she joined in the general conversation and was, thought Kerry sourly, a real asset to the party.

Madeleine irritated her. Probably it was the way she had looked her up and down when they were introduced in the drawing-room just now, as if she didn't think much of the cheesecloth dress. Madeleine's own dress was silvery coloured with the bodice embroidered in gold silk. And now her lips were soft and shining she was quite beautiful. She had smoky blue eyes and delicate cheekbones and her hair fell straight and smooth over her shoulders.

Of course it had to be her room connecting with David's. If she had been in the shower tonight she would probably have glided out slim as a wand and glistening wet. Her skin was pale and he was tanned almost to mahogany, and they would look marvellous together. Kerry was seized with a mad impulse to ask him, 'How did you get that scar on your back?'

Considering she had only peeped through the door for one blink of the eyes the image of a near-naked David Caradoc was fixed in her mind in surprising detail; but if he knew they had shared the bathroom he was unconcerned about it, and although it was a silly thing that would make a funny story, she wasn't going to tell anyone.

She stirred her soup and thought that the dark red of bortsch with its swirling soured cream and sprinkling of green chives probably made it the prettiest soup in the world, and what a pity it was that she hated the taste of beetroot. The only way she could get it down was by taking copious swallows of wine and when David reached to refill her glass she was surprised to find she had almost emptied it.

'Thank you.' She smiled at him briefly and Madeleine said, 'Of course I remember you now. You came into the Galleries on Saturday, didn't you? I thought there was something familiar about you.'

Kerry suspected she had been recognised earlier but Madeleine had been waiting for a lull in the talking so that she could tell the whole table. 'You asked about the Tin Miner, and then you said you didn't like him anyway because you didn't think he would be comfortable to live with.'

There was laughter. Those who didn't know that the Tin Miner was David Caradoc's work were told, and Madeleine put a small delicate hand on his arm and laughed musically. Kerry could imagine her practising that laugh, trilling up and down the scale. Now she was telling David, 'You'll have to change your style, darling.

You're not easy to live with.'

'You can say that again,' said Adrian, 'but she likes my paintings.'

'I'm sure she does,' said David, and they were both smiling, but Kerry felt that David thought she was flattering Adrian, making up to him. Maybe she had been flattering a little.

'I liked almost everything,' she said. 'Some things more than others, of course.'

'The girl has taste,' said Adrian. 'She likes me and the Opie.'

That was the old painting of the bad-tempered woman, and she had only asked about that to change the subject about her buying a house in Penlyn.

'Do tell me about the ones you don't like.' Madeleine laced her fingers beneath her chin and sat looking across at Kerry. 'The public's hard enough to understand, God knows. They shuffle around glassy-eyed, so it would be a help to hear from someone who has decided what she doesn't like. You don't like the Tin Miner, we know that, so what else?'

Kerry was being classed with the glassy-eyed but she ignored the jibe and pretended to give it serious consideration. After a moment she said, 'Well, the Tin Miner was too overpowering for me, but as it wasn't for sale and I probably couldn't afford it if it were, that doesn't count. But there was a picture. Pale blue,' she gestured a square and painted three dots, 'with darker blue balloons, or bubbles, and I thought the price tag on that was a cheek and the title had to be a joke.'

Madeleine's lips thinned again and her simper was definitely forced and Kerry gulped, 'It probably meant something that was beyond me.'

'It probably did,' said Madeleine, in chillier tones. 'It's called "Honesty" because there's no clutter, no deceit, just clean unbroken colour and lines. Nothing pretending to be anything it isn't.'

Incredibly, she was in earnest. She had painted the blue balloons and called them 'Honesty', and Kerry's lips twitched. 'That explains it,' said Kerry. 'I'm all for fantasy. I like make-believe.' There were four of the Players and Erica round the table to agree with her and Madeleine smiled again at David. 'She doesn't appreciate either of us, so I'm in good company.' Her smile changed for Kerry. 'You did know it was one of my pictures, didn't you?'

Kerry hadn't until a minute ago. 'No,' she said.

But they all thought she had. They thought she was sniping back because Madeleine was baiting her, and so did Madeleine who asked, 'What do you do for a living, when you're not being an art critic or an amateur actress?'

'I'm a secretary,' said Kerry, and from the other end of the table Erica protested,

'But what a waste of your talents. You should be on the stage.'

'So should a thousand others,' said Kerry gaily. 'If Penlyn had a pier maybe I could start a concert party.'

'Kerry's out of a job right now,' said Adrian, 'and we think it would be a good thing if she could find something down here.'

'Do we?' Kerry's voice was drowned by other voices. Ruth and Gerald and Jenny and Griff all spoke together. This was a surprise to them and it was a bigger one to Kerry, who had vaguely considered looking for work around Penlyn but had not discussed it with anyone.

'Last night,' said Adrian, 'I said it would be worthwhile asking around and Kerry agreed.' He looked at her fondly and she looked blank for a moment then remembered saying yes, while she was paddling at the sea's edge under the moon, not listening to Adrian, thinking about—David again. 'And she's interested in a cottage in Glenoral Terrace,' Adrian went on. 'Does anyone know anything about it?'

Kerry should have said, 'Hold on,' because she had decided that she couldn't settle in Penlyn. But Erica and Penny knew the terrace and they were well-built nice little houses and they both started talking about them, and David frowned. Only slightly, just a deepening of the line that cut between his brows, but Kerry knew that the prospect of her staying down here displeased him and she wanted to say, 'Tough luck.'

'I always look at estate agents,' she said, and she explained to those who didn't know, 'I've just sold my house and I haven't made up my mind where I'm going to settle.'

'Don't be seduced by Cornwall in weather like this,' said David. 'It's a harsher climate in the winter, and you might get a job in summertime but there's not much work when the tourists have gone.'

That was fair comment, he was telling her nothing she didn't know, but she knew that he disapproved of the way Adrian and Erica had taken to her and he wanted her gone. He must realise it was all play-acting but he had no patience with it and she was blowed if she was going to reassure him. She said, 'I've nearly two weeks left to make up my mind about a house and see what offers I get about a job.'

She laughed at Adrian, exaggeratedly provocative, so that no one could imagine she was being serious, and got smiles all down the table, then she picked up her knife and fork and started on the marinated salmon steak with tiny minted potatoes and grilled courgettes that had replaced her half-empty bowl of bortsch.

The food was delicious. An apricot soufflé and a cheese-board followed the main course, and the wine kept flowing, and Kerry drank several glasses because they helped her put on her own sparkling performance.

Without them she might just have been tongue-tied, inhibited by her slipping neckline and the fact that she was the only woman here wearing a bikini as underwear. Inhibited most of all from practically rubbing shoulders with David Caradoc.

Not that there was any actual contact. They never even brushed hands, she even avoided leaning his way. But you couldn't be in the same room with him, much less at the same table, without sensing the dynamic force of the man. He was good at a dinner-party. He was quietly amused and amusing, with a manner that put everyone at their ease. But without the wine Kerry was not so sure that she would have been easy sitting so close to him.

Adrian was different. He thought she was marvellous, even if it was make-believe. She flirted with Adrian, because that was exactly what he was doing with her, and Ruth's and Jenny's expressions spoke volumes when they caught her eye. Later there would be all sorts of nonsense talked about Kerry's holiday affair with Adrian. She would be teased unmercifully and it certainly was a bit of a giggle, and this was turning into a very amusing evening.

Madeleine smiled a great deal but didn't laugh much, and she gave David so much attention that most of the time Gerald, who was sitting on her right, got a cold shoulder. She didn't seem able to keep her eyes or her hands off David. Silly cow, thought Kerry, as Madeleine missed no chance of touching and brushing, but maybe she needed to press home her claim on him because she surely couldn't be selling many of her paintings if the blue balloons were a typical example.

Kerry would have Louise smiling about that later tonight. And she would have to describe the dining-room, the Gothic lushness of it with its dark red walls and carpets, the silver, the crystal, the paintings. Except for one landscape, that might be a genuine Constable,

most of the paintings were portraits, each with its strip-
lighting, although tonight the only illumination was the
great glittering chandelier, and in pride of place over the
black marble fireplace was Erica. She stood in a high
wind with a background of moors behind her, her
beautiful hair streaming out and her dress moulded and
flowing.

She must have noticed Kerry looking around, turning
in her chair, fixing things in her mind so that she could
tell Louise all about them, because she said, 'I've
changed, haven't I?'

'When was it painted?' Kerry asked.

'Before you were born,' said Erica. 'Before Adrian
was.'

Kerry's surprise was genuine. It looked a slightly
younger Erica, but it could have been a kindly portrait of
her today. 'If you'd said last week,' said Kerry, 'I'd have
believed you.'

'What a lovely thing to say—that is sweet of you,'
Erica said, although she had to know that she still
compared very favourably with her portrait.

Adrian said, 'I want a portrait of Rosalind. How about
it, David? Will you sketch her? Or sculpt her, that would
be even better?'

It was then that Kerry realised that she had been
avoiding looking David Caradoc directly in the face,
because when he drawled, 'Do you think I'd do her
justice?' she had to and it sobered her instantly. The
confidence that the wine and the company had given her
ebbed away, leaving her with a feeling of desperate
insecurity. If he made a subject of her she could imagine
him removing layer after layer until he had stripped away
all the defences she put up against the world. She could
see herself portrayed mercilessly as he probed for her
failings and found them. Deep inside she had doubts and
fears and was lonely and afraid and she would never

allow that to be revealed to those piercing eyes.

Not that he would waste his time and skill on her, although Adrian was asking, 'If she stays on will you?'

'If she stays, maybe,' said David, and to Kerry that was a threat, not a promise, and she said flatly,

'No, thank you. I'd make a rotten subject.'

Several of them said she wouldn't but David looked steadily at her and she felt like a butterfly about to be pinned down, fluttering and panicked, when suddenly Erica said, 'Surely you could find something for Kerry to do in the Galleries, Adrian? And I could use a secretary myself, all these committees, all this paper work.' She was so delighted at the idea that she almost gave herself a round of applause. 'Of *course*,' she said. 'You must work for us, we can keep you busy.'

I wouldn't mind temping for the Caradocs, thought Kerry, at least until the summer ends. Although Erica was obviously inventing jobs for her it was nice to be asked, and she had no doubts that she could make herself useful. But it would put her into an invidious situation because Adrian could be mortally offended if she moved into his galleries and his life and went on holding him off.

'Why did you leave your last post?' asked David quietly.

The Players all knew, of course, and when Kerry said, 'The business closed down,' they realised that she did not want to talk about her bereavement.

'How long were you with them?' He was interviewing her as if she really had applied for a job, he would be wanting references next, and she said,

'Right from secretarial school; I am quite efficient. But this is a holiday and I'll look for a job when the festival ends.'

'Well, the offer stands,' said Erica gaily and David added,

'Let's leave it at that.' He meant, forget it; and that

was Kerry's sentiment too. She was leaving Penlyn with the others so he need not worry about her getting on the Caradoc payroll or seducing his young brother.

Adrian was probably several years older than Kerry but compared with David he seemed very young. She suspected that David always overshadowed him, and she was annoyed at herself for being more aware of David. She liked Adrian more, but even when David wasn't around she still caught herself thinking about him, and when he was near, anatagonism was always just beneath the surface. And there was no pretence about that; it was becoming a gut reaction.

Adrian smiled at her then and she smiled back at him with a gaiety that made him squeeze her fingers; she thought how unforgivable it would be to let this nonsense between herself and Adrian go too far simply to annoy David, because he riled her so much.

But there was no way of recapturing her earlier confidence. That had gone. She was acutely conscious now of her slipping neckline and that she might have been laughing too loud and talking too much. The bikini pants were getting tighter after all that food, cutting into her stomach, and her face felt flushed and hot. When they got up from table Erica said brightly, 'Shall we have a little music?' and Kerry whispered to Adrian, 'I must go.'

Erica swept off, back to the drawing-room, and the dining-room emptied. In the hall Kerry hung back. 'I mean it, it's time I was going.'

'Why don't you stay here?' said Adrian.

'How many rooms do you have?' If he hoped she would share his he was way off the mark but he said,

'There's always another room. This place was built for big families and an army of servants, and most of it's still habitable. Why don't you move in?'

'I'm fine where I am. Besides there's the dog I was

telling you about. He's expecting me back.'

David and Madeleine passed them as they stood at the bottom of the staircase. Madeleine did her flickering glance up and down Kerry, and Kerry shrugged with languid insouciance and David said, 'Your dress is coming off again.'

She had almost shrugged it free from one shoulder, and now she grabbed at it and glared and could have spat at him.

Adrian was smiling and at him Kerry smiled, and told him how she had taken the drawstring out to make it more like a dress for a dinner-party. 'I should have practised moving about in it before I came downstairs, because it's either looser or I'm slippier than I thought. And why didn't you tell me this was a party tonight?'

'Did it matter?'

'Look at me.' She was still holding her neckline together and he said,

'I'm looking and I think you're lovely.'

'Your brother thinks I'm a slob, so does Madeleine, and that was even before I made the crack about her painting. I didn't know it was hers by the way, I remember the initials, I read them, N.B.'

'M. Madeleine Brenner. And she is quite well thought of.'

She just stopped herself shrugging again. 'I still think she should knock a nought off the price she's asking. Anyhow, thanks for a lovely meal, I'll collect my bag and be on my way.'

He went up with her, to Ruth and Gerald's room, and inside the room with its intimate atmosphere of the bed and discarded garments she scooped up her beach-bag quickly.

'I wouldn't make the same mistake twice in two days,' he said. 'Grabbing you on the beach and in the bedroom.'

'Of course you wouldn't,' she had to smile, 'you've

much too much sense.'

'Not that I don't want to.' He sounded wistful rather than passionate, and she knew that she would have no problem with Adrian that she couldn't cope with. At least for two weeks, and beyond that she would have other problems a long way away.

The drawstring lay on the dressing-table and she grimaced at her reflection in the mirror. She looked as though she had been blown in on a high wind, and she couldn't get the drawstring back in the dress without taking the dress off. She delved into her beach-bag and came up triumphantly with a safety pin that would hold her together while she walked across the foyer of Wayside. She was getting weary of perpetually hitching up.

The pin went through the material with a jerk, pricking her thumb, and she yelped and Adrian said, 'Come here, let me.'

He was fastening the pin, his fingers trembling slightly, and Kerry was about to say, 'Thank you', and move away when there was a gasp from the open doorway. Ruth was framed there. She had been walking in but now swayed backwards, babbling apologies, 'Sorry, excuse me, I came to get——' She looked as though she had completely forgotten what she had come for. Her lips twitched in a smile of acute embarrassment. 'So sorry,' she mumbled and turned and fled down the carpeted corridor.

By the time Kerry was at the door calling, 'I left my bag in here,' Ruth had rounded the corner, and anyhow what else could Kerry say? 'He was pinning my dress together'?

'It doesn't take much to shock her,' said Adrian.

'Usually she's very broad-minded,' said Kerry. 'She didn't expect to find anybody in here, and from where she was standing——'

She began to laugh, and after a moment Adrian joined in.

'I should be so lucky. You're sure you want to go back to Wayside?'

Her lips curved and her eyes danced. 'Get me out of this house. My reputation's in tatters as it is.'

She could have walked back but when he crossed to the garages she raised no objection. Getting into the car, she looked up at all the lighted windows and said inanely, 'It's a big house,' and then, 'Does Madeleine live here?'

'No. She stays sometimes.' And Kerry knew which room she had. She said, keeping her voice light and amused,

'You said she was after David. I should have thought she had got him.'

'Oh, no,' Adrian sounded sure of that, and they swept down the drive that curved past the lawn with the great stones and through the gateway.

He turned on the radio as Kerry said, 'I hear you were engaged. What happened there?'

'She got a better offer.'

No big deal, Louise had been told, and that was how it sounded, rueful but not bitter. 'I'm sorry,' she said.

'I'm not,' said Adrian.

On the radio was a programme of folk songs, and she hummed the tunes and sang a line here and there as they drove through the still-busy streets. The Festival meant plenty of evening entertainments. 'I know where I'm going,' she sang softly, and thought how wrong that was when she couldn't see the way at all, much less who was going with her.

'Why go anywhere?' said Adrian. 'Why don't you stay here? Erica was right, there is a job in the Galleries. The artists have always helped out but we can use another permanent assistant.' It was hard to explain why not and while she hesitated he said, 'Come and try it tomorrow morning.'

That could do no harm. 'Maybe,' she said, and he drew up in front of Wayside and told her, 'I shall be watching the play tomorrow afternoon.'

'Who'll be watching the store?'

'Adam. Anybody. I might have to close the doors but I won't miss Rosalind.'

'It's fun to have a fan club,' she said, and he kissed her hand because she was already half out of the car.

She had a fan club of two. Coco leapt on her in the hall and padded after her upstairs. The bedroom was dark and empty and before she pressed the light-switch she stood for a moment, leaning against the wall. It had been a fun-packed evening, so why did Kerry feel as if the lights were out all over the world? She was missing her father, of course, and tonight had not been fun, not really, not all of it. When David Caradoc had looked at her she had felt her loneliness like a life sentence.

In the shadows her fingers touched the dog's short silky coat and she stroked him and said, 'Know what I'd like to do? Crawl into bed and cry my eyes out.' Instead she turned on the lights, undressed and washed and when Louise came in about half an hour later she regaled her with a hilarious account of dining out in Maen Bos.

Louise loved it all: the dress that kept slipping off, the painting called 'Honesty', Ruth walking into her bedroom and finding Kerry and Adrian in what seemed like a passionate clinch. She laughed until tears rolled down her cheeks and then she said, 'Go on, you've left the best bit out.'

All Kerry had left out was David Caradoc, and he was not the best bit, he was the worst. 'Like what?' she asked.

'Fastening a pin my foot,' said Louise. 'Oh, I am pleased. Is it the real thing, do you think? Oh, wouldn't that be romantic?'

'Wouldn't it?' said Kerry, and knew there was no chance at all because the last thing she wanted was any kind of commitment . . .

Next morning she did go down to the Galleries. She was not looking for a permanent job but while she was here it might be interesting to learn something about the background of a fine arts gallery. How they operated, put on exhibitions; and meeting customers and artists might be fun.

Robin had teased her over breakfast. Louise got down a minute or two before Kerry and she must have used the time telling him what happened to Kerry last night, with her own and Ruth's interpretation of the bedroom scene, because he grinned widely and said, 'I hear there were wild goings-on in the ancestral home.'

'An orgy,' said Kerry. 'There was this fantastic chandelier and Gerald was swinging on it and lobbing grapes down Penny Penrose's front.'

'That as well?' said Rob. 'Well, good on you. You did say, didn't you, you wouldn't mind settling for Maen Bos?'

'Nobody's offered me that,' said Kerry, 'but I have been offered a couple of jobs. Secretary to Erica and lend a hand in the Galleries.' She hadn't mentioned that to Louise, who now opened her eyes very wide.

Rob gasped, 'The family's accepted you! Good lord, it is serious!'

'No, it isn't,' said Kerry, and the memory of David came at her as clearly as if he were standing there. David Caradoc had not accepted her. He was not in favour of anything that kept her in Penlyn, although it was no concern of his what she did. And he certainly couldn't stop her going into the Galleries this morning.

She parted from Louise and Rob on the sea-front. They had decided on a boat trip and were off to consult the list chalked up outside the little booking-office, but they all reached the Galleries together and Kerry said, 'See you up at Maen Bos around one.'

'Behave yourself,' said Rob.

'He's a fine one to talk about behaving yourself,' said Louise. 'You be a devil and enjoy yourself,' and she waited to see Kerry go through the door and Adrian come hurrying from the back of the shop to meet her. Then she linked arms with Robin and asked him, 'Do you think Kerry will stay down here?'

'She hasn't got much to go back to, has she?' said Rob.

'Not really,' Louise had to agree, and she thought of their own sweet little house and Rob's secure and steady job, and watched Kerry through the glass door, walking down the gallery with Adrian's arm around her shoulders. 'I wonder if David Caradoc was there last night,' she said, 'she never mentioned him.'

'Then I shouldn't think he was,' said Rob, drawing her away. 'He isn't a man you'd overlook.'

It was good to be greeted, Kerry thought. Adrian seemed so pleased to see her and she was pleased to see him, and his arm guiding her was light and friendly. The Galleries could provide a job, although there was a woman and a man helping out this morning as well as Adrian. Vicky, who was nervously thin and intense, had one of the easels upstairs. Several of them used that studio, it must be a busy little centre of activity, and Kerry could have fitted in: serving customers, making coffee, helping with clerical work. But she couldn't stay beyond the run of the play so this was just part of her holiday.

When Adrian introduced her as Rosalind it seemed to sum up the situation. It gave her a status because Vicky had been in Saturday's audience and thought Rosalind was terrific, and as a sort of artist herself Kerry was immediately accepted. But it did make her conscious that she was playing a part, and that was fine because it was a happy role. She was a girl having a wonderful time, enjoying herself, and on the whole it was true.

The one small blot on her morning in the Galleries was the Tin Miner. That bust on its plinth did dominate, and she found herself giving it a wide berth as if it generated some sinister force. But everybody else seemed to admire it. The tourists all gravitated to it before they started wandering around looking at everything else, and it appeared that David Caradoc was a master of his craft.

Vicky was staggered when Kerry said that she had never heard of him before she came to Penlyn. They were eating doughnuts up in the studio, around eleven o'clock, and Vicky had been asking how long she had known Adrian, who had made no secret of his admiration that morning. 'Since Saturday,' Kerry had said.

'You'd have seen David's work, though.' Vicky was taking that for granted until Kerry said she had never heard of him and then Vicky gasped, 'But he's very successful and very well known. He's in galleries and museums all over the world. And in private collections, of course.'

'I seem to have missed him.' said Kerry and Vicky looked pityingly at her.

She left for Maen Bos ahead of Adrian, walking up with an hour in hand to change and make-up and prepare, pre-performance nerves already tightening in her stomach. The buffet lunch in the kitchens seemed to be a regular feature and the small parlour was set aside again as a meeting-place for the actors before they moved into the changing-tent.

Erica was doing them proud. She was sitting on a sofa now, holding court, and when she saw Kerry she stretched out a regal hand. The queen was in her parlour, thought Kerry, maybe I should curtsey. '*Helloo*,' said Erica, in a voice husky with meaning. 'Is Adrian with you?'

'He's still in the Galleries. He says he is coming to see the play again.'

'I should hope so,' said Erica, and she patted Kerry's hand and laughed a little.

Ruth had to be put right about last night and Kerry looked around for her but Ruth was already at her elbow murmuring, 'There's a little thing I want to tell you about your costume,' as she led her out of the room.

As soon as they reached a spot where they were out of anyone else's hearing Kerry began, 'About last night——' and Ruth said, 'I'm terribly sorry.'

'You didn't disturb anything. You didn't break anything up, there wasn't anything going on. I left my bag in your bedroom and I needed a pin in the neck of my dress and Adrian was fastening it for me.'

'Yes, of course,' said Ruth, who obviously thought she had rarely heard a more unlikely tale. 'But—well the fact of the matter is I came downstairs rather confused and almost at once somebody, I think it was Jenny, said "Where's Kerry?" and I said——' She covered her face with one hand, horrified at her own blunder. 'I said "Oh, I'm sure they'll be down soon," and I think everybody must have heard because it went quiet and I know I was turning bright red, and then everyone started talking at once. But then neither of you came back and—oh, I am sorry. It was none of my business, you're a big girl and he seems a nice young man, but oh, what a stupid, tactless thing to say.'

'He was fastening a pin,' said Kerry, and Ruth nodded, but Kerry knew she was still convinced that she had stumbled into an erotic and private situation. It would have been better if Ruth had kept her mouth shut, but there was nothing Kerry could do about that now. Erica didn't seem to be bothered, and it didn't much matter if the rest presumed that Kerry and Adrian were holiday lovers. They weren't and they were not going to be, but folk believed what they wanted to believe and if this spice of scandal entertained them, fair enough.

'It's all right,' said Kerry. 'It really doesn't matter.'

There was a large audience again that afternoon. Word of mouth was doing the advertising because by now the whole of Penlyn and a fair area around knew that *As You Like It* in the Caradoc gardens was well worth the ticket price.

It was a joy to play Rosalind. As soon as Kerry stepped on to the velvet turf her stage-fright vanished and she entered an enchanted world. All the company felt the same, they knew they would probably never again have such a perfect setting for their play and they all gave their roles extra zing and vitality, so that Gerald Harris looked at them quite moist-eyed with pride when they were taking their bows.

Adrian was waiting for Kerry outside the changing-tent like a stage-door fan, and she almost had an argument when she insisted on going back to Wayside to walk the dog, instead of returning to the Galleries with him. 'I can't bear to let you out of my sight,' he said, 'I'm scared you'll vanish into the shadows.' But once outside the gates she headed her own way, after placating him by promising to be waiting for him at seven and that they could spend the evening together again.

They ate and danced at a hotel with a swimming-pool like a lagoon, and again Adrian was well known and Kerry had a fantastic time. So, it seemed, did Adrian. She kept him talking and smiling, and when he took her back to Wayside he said, 'You'll come down to the Galleries tomorrow morning?'

She had enjoyed this morning but she told him again, 'I'm not looking for a job yet, I'm on holiday.'

'I know,' he said. 'Two weeks less two days, and that's why I want every minute of it with you.'

He was almost as good as his word. From then on they

spent enough of each day together to qualify as a pair. All the locals heard that Adrian Caradoc was going around with the girl who was playing Rosalind. That brought some to see the play who otherwise might not have bothered, and having seen Kerry they went away agreeing that the girl could certainly act.

The Players were on the whole tickled pink. Kerry was popular and they had all been sorry for her when her father had died. Some hoped she wasn't going to be hurt, because the Caradocs were obviously filthy rich and Adrian Caradoc could be a raving womaniser for all they knew. But as Louise told them all, Kerry was keeping her head. 'She knows this won't last, she isn't taking it seriously,' and, reassured by that, most of her colleagues looked tolerantly on her romance.

Kerry was grateful to Adrian. Less because he was spoiling her and spending money on her—that bothered her, often she insisted on paying her share—than because he helped to fill her days so completely. He had accepted the proviso about her nights. It became like a joke between them, he trying to persuade her to move into Maen Bos and her inevitable refusal. They both knew she was staying in her own bed, and although everyone was convinced they were lovers their kisses always stopped long before the point of no return. But thanks to Adrian Caradoc, who called her Rosalind and made her feel like Rosalind, she was having a marvellously escapist holiday far removed from real life.

Sometimes she could even pretend that her father was still alive, running the driving-school and living in the house that had been the only home she could remember. And that she had just sent him a postcard, 'Having a wonderful time, wish you were here.' Oh, how she wished he were here! Or anywhere else in this world. But nobody spoke about her father, all her friends thought she was getting over his death nicely, and she spoke about him to no one.

Except Coco. The dog expected her now, after the afternoon performance. 'I swear that dratted animal's learning to tell the time,' said Mr Hayle, and after the first week Kerry couldn't disappoint him. Most of the company were convinced that she was dashing off to be with Adrian, who dropped her at Wayside most afternoons with fairly good grace.

She and the dog always walked on the downs. The streets and the beaches were congested but the moors had no limits they were likely to reach in an hour or so's march, and she was learning her way around. She made landmarks of rocks and trees, burned patches from summer fires and the occasional darker lusher green covering oozing water.

And the old road was always there. She liked the old road so much that she could rarely resist drifting back to it even if she didn't follow it all the way to the mine. She explained to Coco why she kept away from the mine. She talked to the dog when there were no other walkers in sight. She didn't want to come on David Caradoc again if he should be working in that other studio of his. She would always keep her distance from David Caradoc, although every day when she stepped out to play her part on the lawns of Maen Bos she scanned the audience for his face. Adrian thought she was looking for him, and he was usually there. So was Erica, but Kerry knew that David Caradoc had never watched a second performance, and that was a relief because he did her no good.

They met three times in nearly two weeks, but when anyone came over to a table where Kerry and Adrian were sitting, or when they were greeted by somebody Adrian knew, the first objective obviously was to get a look at Kerry. This affair was being talked about even if the gossips only knew half the story. But almost always they then said, 'Remember me to David,' before they went, so his name came up regularly.

Once he came into the Galleries, and once she was in the hall of Maen Bos with a group of Players when he strolled across and that quiet-spoken self-assurance of his made her behave outrageously. He treated her with casual amusement, as if he knew that Adrian considered her special and thought the idea was ridiculous. In front of David Caradoc she overacted, over-reacted, and although nobody else seemed to notice when her voice got shriller she was was convinced that he did.

The third time was on the last Thursday evening. For the previous two days the weather had been erratic. There was still sunshine, but cooler winds had been creeping up and darker clouds appearing in the sky. Thursday's performance was played in a distinct drop in temperature, and rain began to fall during the final scene and that was when Erica decided there should be a rehearsal in Maen Bos in case it was impossible to put on the play outside tomorrow.

The Players were sorry to be leaving their own forest of Arden but the festival was nearing its end. They were stimulated by the prospect of acting in the big hall, and Kerry had fancied coming down that sweeping staircase as Rosalind from the first day. There was plenty of noise and chatter and bustle going on. Gerald was working out scenes and shouting instructions, and Erica was deciding what plants should be brought in from the conservatory to represent a wood, when David walked along the gallery where Kerry was standing.

He stood, looking down at Erica waving in a great potted palm under which Rob was staggering, and Kerry could understand his exasperation because it looked like a madhouse. 'Don't worry,' she said, 'we'll all be gone by Sunday.'

'Can I rely on that?' he said grimly, and perversely

then she had to grin and say,

'Not entirely.'

He strode off, back the way he had come, and very soon there was order out of chaos. But before Gerald was satisfied he made them go over their parts again and again, and then he gave them their orders. If tomorrow's weather was unsettled they were to report here at eleven o'clock in the morning. Then it would be decided where they would be putting on the play. If it was indoors he wanted their performances adjusted in every detail to this unusual theatre, and also he wanted them to help put out the chairs.

It rained all night. Kerry woke and heard it pattering on the window panes and lay awake because then she started thinking. She would have to leave with the others, but she would be sorry to go, and what about Coco? It was silly to have let herself get so attached to an animal that wasn't hers, but the thought of him being abandoned twice gave her a pang of regret. She would go back and buy a small house or flat and find a job near all her friends, but she didn't think that she wanted to do that. She didn't really know what she did want, as she lay tossing, listening to the rain. But that was nothing new, there had not been much purpose in her life for months . . .

'Well, this settles it,' said Louise sitting up and pulling a face. 'Beastly weather.'

Compared with the days of sunshine it was, but Kerry had already been outside and when the wind dropped it was still warm. Unfortunately the rain seemed to have settled into a fine persistent drizzle. The ground would be soaked and there was no sign of blue in the grey sky, so it was off to Maen Bos to be put through their paces again.

Louise was not really disappointed. She was looking forward to acting on the gallery and the staircase and the small section of hall they had set aside as part of the stage. This meant a decreased audience but no one would have paid to sit outside on a day like this and it was all going to be cosy and intimate.

Gerald continued to rehearse his company, while Penny Penrose, under the eagle eye of a Fire Prevention Officer, organised benches and seats and chairs, and by the time the doors were opened to the ticket holders the cast were in full costume and make-up.

It went well. Gestures had to be restrained, there was less moving around, but they all remembered which was the palace and which was the wood, and the acting was good. David Caradoc watched this time, standing at the back, and after her first glance in his direction Kerry never looked at him again. But she played her part with all her heart and at the end when Rosalind and Orlando came hand in hand down the great staircase to join the rest of the cast there was a standing ovation.

In spite of his shortsightedness, Robin had managed nearly two weeks negotiating cables and avoiding trees without putting a foot wrong, but half-way down the staircase of Maen Bos he stumbled and lurched, and only saved himself by clutching the handrail like a drowning man. It was Kerry, thrown off balance and hampered by her flowing skirts, who went rolling down.

There was silence while she fell. For a matter of seconds everyone was dumbstruck, but as she landed at the bottom a babble of concern rose to shrieking crescendo. The costume that had tripped her had also cushioned her and her immediate reaction was to try to get up. Robin had come rushing down the stairs, carrying on as if everyone would accuse him of doing this deliberately. 'I don't know how it happened, Kerry, are you all right? I must have missed the step.' Louise and Ruth had an arm each and while the rest of the cast milled around Kerry stood up, then crumpled as an ankle gave way with a stab of pain. That was a legacy from a school sports-day, and an awkward landing over the high jump. She had almost forgotten it, it had given her no trouble for years, but if she turned her foot sharply or went over on it there could be a twinge from the weak spot.

Adrian and Erica had been in the front row and when Adrian dashed in to support her the others let him. He picked her up as she sagged against Ruth, and it had been a frightening fall, tumbling headlong, enmeshed in the long red velvet skirts, bouncing down from stair to stair. She was badly shaken and it was comforting to be gathered up and carried in Adrian's arms, and she turned her face into his shoulder and put her arms round his neck, closing her eyes and trying to stop shaking.

The audience was hastily ushered out, chattering excitedly. One ghoulish voice reached Kerry. 'Nasty, wasn't it? A fall like that could cripple her.' And somebody else was asking somebody, 'Do you remember that scene in *Gone With the Wind* when she fell down the staircase?' as though it was some kind of contest—who fell farther, Scarlett or Rosalind?

Adrian gently laid her down on a sofa in the drawing-room and when she opened her eyes she thought that his face must be whiter than her own. He looked in a terrible state, and Louise, on the edge of tears, knelt down beside her, begging for reassurance, 'Are you all right? Oh, Kerry, that was so awful.'

As soon as she got her breath Kerry croaked, 'Yes, I am all right.'

'Rob's frantic.' Louise almost sobbed. 'He feels terrible, slipping and shoving you and then letting you go.'

'They'd have loved to see the two of us rolling down together,' said Kerry, slightly hysterically. 'Really, I am all right.'

A doctor who had been in the audience examined her

and then told her what she could have told him, that there were no bones broken. The ankle might need a little support for a while and she should rest to make sure there were no after-effects.

All the time Adrian paced up and down the room, in a state of acute anxiety, Rob was apologising to anybody who would listen to him, and the whole company appeared to be gathered around the sofa. When the doctor ordered rest he added, 'And quiet, for an hour or so,' and then the room began to empty.

David Caradoc left with the doctor and Erica said, 'You'll stay here, of course. I'll have a room prepared. Rest for a while and then we'll get you into it.'

'That's right,' babbled Adrian. 'You lie still, you'll be all right. Oh my poor little darling.'

So Kerry lay still, counting her blessings. She could have ended up in a bad way but instead she was almost sure that a few bruises and a twinge or two from her ankle would be the sum total of her injuries. A few bruises on the first night I came here and a few more at the end of my run, she thought wryly, and David Caradoc came back into the room and walked across to where she lay.

She was still shaking. Watching him she got the sensation of falling again, the same quaking hollow of fear in her stomach, and she thought—I'm still in shock.

'Drink this,' he said.

The room was empty. Fancy leaving me alone with him, she thought woozily. It should be Ruth or Louise bringing me whatever I have to drink. 'What is it?' she asked.

'Only a sedative. The doctor left it. Nobody's drugging you.'

'Where is everybody?'

'Who do you want?'

'Nobody. But the room was full a minute ago.'

'About ten minutes ago,' he said. 'They'll all be

flocking back any time. The actors are getting out of their costumes. Erica is organising a sick-room for you, and Adrian has gone to gather roses.'

'What?' She gulped down the glass of brackish-looking liquid and wondered if her hearing had been affected.

'To put in your room,' said David.

'Goodness,' she said, and then, 'It's a kind thought.'

He gave her a cool weighing look and said, 'You were lucky. You must be a tough lady.'

She could feel antagonism filling the hollow, her fighting spirit coming back. 'I'll still have a few bruises to take away with me,' she said. 'The early ones faded. I see the mark on your eye did too.'

He didn't smile and neither did she. He was looking at her as though she was still an intruder and she said, 'Sorry if I'm causing trouble.'

'Are you?'

'I didn't fall down your stairs for laughs. I might be an exhibitionist but that would be going over the top.'

She was not an exhibitionist. Acting was a different thing. In her private life her reserve was deep, but he always made her say things like that.

'I hope you aren't going to cause trouble,' he said.

'Do you now?'

'Up to now,' he said, 'this affair between you and Adrian has been mildly diverting.'

'A laugh a minute,' she said, and decided that one of her brightest memories from these two weeks could be the punch she swung at him. She wouldn't mind doing that again any time.

'You're probably an even better actress than Erica,' he said, 'and I shouldn't like to see my brother making as big a fool of himself as my father did. He's gone to pieces over this fall of yours.'

'Well, I'm *sorry*,' she said savagely, 'but I'm sure he'll recover as quickly as I shall, and I don't call a little concern nor a few roses picked from the garden going to pieces. I'd have shared my sedative with him if you'd mentioned it sooner,' and she set the empty glass down on the carpet.

'So long as that's all you're planning on sharing,' said David Caradoc, and there was no mistaking the grimness in his voice and his eyes, 'because he has just told me he is going to marry you.'

CHAPTER FIVE

KERRY nearly burst out laughing, because that was absurd. She had no desire to marry anyone for a long time and she had never considered Adrian as the man with whom she wanted to share her life. 'Of course he isn't,' she was going to say when David Caradoc said,

'Which would be a big mistake for both of you,' and he was threatening her, there was no mistake about that. He was towering over her, and he must be well over six feet tall, arrogant as Lucifer, and she was damned if she would agree meekly with anything he said. Of course it was crazy but David Caradoc was not going back to his brother making Adrian look a fool, telling him that Kerry had said so.

Adrian couldn't be serious, but if for the moment he was, Kerry would have to explain that he didn't know her at all and that if he did he wouldn't want to marry her.

She wished she were on her feet. Even then she would have had to tilt her head to look David Caradoc in the eyes, but lying flat out on the sofa made her feel vulnerable and the sedative was having a surprisingly quick effect. 'That is your opinion,' she said, and she hoped she was conveying that she couldn't care less for his opinion. 'I'll wait until I'm asked and then I'll decide if it would be a mistake,' and she closed her eyes.

But it was hard to breathe naturally with him only a hand's stretch away. She could sense him, almost see him through her closed lids glaring down at her, the shape of his mouth and jaw-line, the texture of his skin, the way the hair grew back from his forehead, dark hair with the tawny touch where the light caught it.

She had shut him out, dismissed him, and she was sure that hardly ever happened. She expected him to say something more to make her open her eyes again, even touch her. He would probably like to shake her, but he would hardly go that far, and whatever he did she would mumble, 'Go away, I have to rest.'

He must move quietly for such a big man and it was a thick carpet, because after a minute when she squinted up through her lashes the room was empty. The sedative seemed to have stopped working, or perhaps it hadn't started. Perhaps there was a force field around David Caradoc that played havoc with her metabolism. If he had touched her she could well have shot up like somebody electrocuted and it was a relief to find herself alone. Right from the fight on that first night she had had this fear that this man might destroy her.

Destroy was a big word. Not a word to apply to someone you had only met fleetingly, because she would be gone from here the day after tomorrow. But the fall had taken her strength away, and the sedative was putting her into the state, before sleep, when the mind can clear briefly and the truth emerges. And the truth was that he scared the life out of her.

She had never been frightened of anybody before. She had known fear, loneliness, sadness, but she had never met anyone who had made her want to turn and run. I should not have taken that sedative, she thought. I'm all right. I should not be lying here. I've broken nothing, but now I shall probably be dopey for hours. Perhaps he's poisoned me. And that was a suggestion to make anyone smile, it was so ridiculous, but she found herself sniffing as if tears were not far away, and just then Louise came in, all signs of Celia removed.

'How are you?' Louise asked. She was still anxious and when Kerry said,

'I'm muzzy. I've had a sedative,' she nodded.

'I know. They've got a room ready for you.'

'I don't need a room.' But she couldn't lie on the sofa in the drawing-room all evening, the others were coming back, and she had to get out of the Rosalind costume and make-up. She could not doze in here, so the obvious thing was a handy bed.

'Don't stand on it,' said Ruth sharply. Ruth was a district nurse, and she had Kerry supported across the hall to one of the rooms leading off. 'Right now,' said Ruth when she had ushered out everyone but Louise, 'let's have a look at that ankle.'

'I'm a fraud,' said Kerry. 'It is a weak ankle and I turned it but it hardly hurts at all, and there's nothing else the matter.'

'Thank heaven for that,' said Louise fervently. 'Adrian Caradoc has been carrying on as if you're going to be confined to a wheelchair. When he heard that Rob was shortsighted he had a real go at him. Anyone would think Rob tripped you up on purpose.' Louise's pretty face was mutinous, she had gone off Adrian. 'Didn't he create?' She turned to Ruth for confirmation and Ruth said drily,

'I don't know how that young man would be in a real emergency.'

'David told him not to be so stupid,' said Louise, as though she had enjoyed that. 'The girl isn't hurt,' he said. Adrian wouldn't believe us but he shut up fast enough when David spoke to him.'

Neither of them seemed to know that Adrian had said he was going to marry Kerry so he must have told David when they were alone, and that to David was the ultimate stupidity. That had brought him into the drawing-room, with the sedative and a threat that was not even veiled. Althought what big brother could do, except disapprove, Kerry could not imagine; and she had to stop feeling that David Caradoc could break her.

'Pretty room,' she said. It was a little sitting-room-cum-bedroom with a Chinese décor: black lacquered furniture and exquisitely painted silk panels on the wall. A single bed, with scarlet peonies on the magnolia quilt, was turned down, and a door opened into a cloakroom.

Louise helped her out of her costume. She wasn't fighting the drowsiness, she needed to rest. She removed her theatrical make-up and Ruth bandaged her ankle with a deft professional touch.

'I'd have been livelier without the sedative,' said Kerry with a great yawn. 'Don't you clear off and leave me here. You wake me before you go.'

'Erica says you're staying,' Ruth said.

'We're fetching you an overnight bag,' said Louise, and there was a tap on the door and Louise opened it on Adrian behind a bunch of roses.

'How is she?' he asked, peering in for a glimpse of Kerry.

'Resting,' said Louise coldly. 'She'll live.' She took the flowers and swayed slightly, so that he could see Kerry sitting on the side of the bed although Louise was still blocking his way in.

'I'm fine,' Kerry called. 'Just fine.'

'As you were told,' said Louise. 'So there was no need to rave at Robin like that. It was an accident and he was upset enough.'

Adrian ignored her. 'I picked roses without thorns,' he told Kerry and Louise said,

'Very nice,' and shut the door.

Ruth and Kerry were smiling. Louise was usually a placid girl but now she looked like a small ruffled hen. 'Well,' she said, and began to grin, pleased that she had slammed the door on the man who had made such a fuss when they were all feeling upset. 'I'm sure he thinks a lot of you but I think he's a wimp. He's not a patch on his brother.'

'What's his brother got to do with it?' asked Ruth, and

Louise picked up a Chinese vase and took it into the cloakroom to fill it with water and roses.

'Just saying I know which Caradoc I'd leave home for,' she said and giggled and it was a joke. Ruth laughed and Kerry pretended to laugh. Adrian had found her roses without thorns, and when she was with Adrian she felt smooth and graceful and scented. It was with David that she felt like a spiky prickly cactus.

'Watch that vase,' she said. 'It's probably Ming something-or-other and worth a fortune.'

She slept heavily and when she woke it was a few seconds before she realised where she was. The first thing she saw were these strange birds with feathers that were tipped with gold. Then she saw that they were painted on a screen, and that Louise was standing by the door.

'All right?' asked Louise, still sounding worried, and Kerry sat up at once to reassure her.

'Oh, yes. It was the sedative that knocked me out, not the fall. Honestly, no trouble at all.' She stuck out her foot and wriggled her ankle in its swathing of bandages. 'Not even this. What time is it?'

There was a light on. That must have woken her. 'Just after nine,' said Louise. 'Ruth's been looking in on you and she said to let you sleep it off.'

'Sounds like a hangover.'

'There'll be a few of them tomorrow,' said Louise. 'We were all invited to stay and the wine's been flowing like water. We're celebrating.'

Kerry gulped. 'Celebrating what?'

'Well, we have done well, practically a sell-out every afternoon. Several of us are driving home tomorrow, so tonight's a good time to have a farewell party I suppose. And the committee are very pleased with us. Erica in particular.'

For a dismayed moment Kerry had thought that the celebration might be to do with her and Adrian. But of course it wasn't. He might have told David his intentions, although she felt that that was just an impulsive spur-of-the-moment remark; and he certainly wouldn't be making announcements without talking to her.

She had been lying on top of the bed, dressed. Her shoes stood near and she managed to get the left one on over her bandage. She brushed her hair and put on lipstick and a blusher before a wall mirror, and assured Louise that she would be able to play Rosalind for the Players' swansong tomorrow afternoon.

'I tell you what,' said Louise, 'after this I'm going to make him persevere with contact lenses, because he could have killed the pair of you. Either that or wear his glasses twenty-four hours a day.'

Rob was wearing his glasses in the drawing-room now. Behind their horn rims his eyes were mournful as he came hurrying to Kerry's side, full of apologies. She laughed, stretching the truth a little, and told him, 'I don't even have a bruise. That velvet gown was like falling downstairs wrapped in a blanket.'

But before Rob could speak Adrian snatched her away. 'Your ankle's bandaged. How's your ankle?'

She was walking on it but he almost carried her back to the sofa which cleared as they approached, when Gerald and Penny Penrose's husband who had been sitting there talking cricket got up. Feeling a sham, Kerry was ceremoniously set down by Adrian, and her feet lifted to take up almost the full length of the sofa in spite of her protests.

'Thank God you are all right,' said Adrian, 'but you need looking after,' and he sat at her feet, staring soulfully into her eyes. We must look a right couple of idiots, she thought. Everybody seemed to be smiling. Louise caught Kerry's glance and rolled her eyes, and then Kerry saw David.

He was some way away, across the room, standing in the middle of a group, with that sardonic expression she had seen before. But this time she knew that it masked anger. He was holding a glass, and she watched him put it down with a steady hand and thought, he's angry enough to smash that and then yank Adrian to his feet.

'I shouldn't like to see my brother making as big a fool of himself as my father did,' he had said, and he believed that this relationship was becoming serious and that Kerry was a second Erica, who must always have been a very demanding lady. She almost wished she could fall in love with Adrian just to prove that she was not anything like Erica. What Adrian felt for her was make-believe, once reality crept in it wouldn't last beyond a few weeks, but he was making a fool of himself now.

She wished he would stop fussing, and she said, 'Don't fuss,' but it didn't do much good. He was set on treating her like a convalescent. When she put her feet down he put them up again, and she had to wait until he went to fetch her a drink before she could take up less room on the sofa and stop looking like Madame Recamier.

Louise brought her a plate of sandwiches. After breakfast Kerry rarely ate much before the afternoon performance, and tonight she had missed an evening meal, but she wasn't particularly hungry. She nibbled the sandwiches, sipping her wine and joining in the talk which was mostly about the festival. It had been quite a success and their ticket returns had amply justified Erica's confidence in shipping them down to act *As You Like It* in her garden.

'What I would dearly like,' said Erica, happily lit with champagne, 'is a little theatre, here in Maen Bos. And that isn't such an impossible dream. One of the outhouses could be converted, perhaps the old coach-house. Local people could use it, and you could all come down during the summer season, couldn't you?'

Of course they could, they said. 'Kerry could stay and help me,' said Erica gaily. 'She did say that if Penlyn had a pier she'd start a concert party.'

This was all cloud-cuckoo talk and Kerry smiled, and Louise asked, 'Isn't Kerry coming back with us?'

'She's staying here and marrying me,' said Adrian.

Silence again. The same hush that had fallen when she fell down the stairs, and then the voices, not shrieking this time, just gasping and babbling.

Adrian held her hand and he was saying, 'Aren't you, my Rosalind?' and she couldn't believe that he was creating a scene like this in front of a whole roomful of spectators.

She looked away and her eyes met David's again and for a moment his anger scorched her, then the shutters came down and his face became inscrutable. No one else noticed. Everyone else was staring at her and Adrian, but she dared not look in David's direction again.

'Rosalind has had enough excitement for one day,' she said desperately and Adrian said,

'I'm not joking. I mean it.'

'Me too,' she said, and to Erica, 'I wonder you don't open a little theatre. Think of the fun you could have. You could start your own company. Our Playhouse used to be an old cinema. It was quite derelict, you should see the old photographs. Gerald was in right from the beginning, he could give you some tips.'

They were reluctant to let the marriage proposal be shelved. Adrian Caradoc had just asked Kerry to marry him, seriously and in front of thirty or so witnesses, and she was never going to turn him down when she had no home and no family and no prospects. And he was wealthy and good-looking and mad about her.

She knew it was being discussed in whispers all round the room and she could have stood up and shouted, 'He doesn't mean it. He doesn't know the first thing about

me, and I couldn't marry him. I'd sooner pitch tent on a
desert island than move into Maen Bos.'

Adrian couldn't have stopped to think at all. He was
like his mother. She had suddenly decided she wanted to
build her own little theatre, he thought he wanted his
Rosalind for ever. They were like a couple of impulsive
and charming children, but they were both kind and she
couldn't slap him down in front of them all. Later,
quietly, she would make it clear that this had been a
holiday romance which they both knew had no future.

So she smiled and talked and drank a glass of
champagne and said, 'No comment,' when anyone tried
to talk about Adrian's proposal. It was a joke, she would
tell them tomorrow. And he could say that too, so his
pride need not be hurt; and for all she knew it might be a
joke although he had held her hand tight when he had
said, 'I mean it.'

Louise was probably right about there being a few
hangovers in the morning because the party was fizzing.
Everybody seemed to be enjoying themselves and the
room appeared to be getting fuller and the voices louder,
and Kerry's bruises began to ache. When Ruth asked,
'Are you all right?' she had to admit, 'I'm a bit tired.'

Adrian was temporarily away from her. He had said,
'Ask Rosalind,' while she was saying, 'No comment,' but
across the room she had no idea what he was telling
them. David had gone some time ago. She wasn't looking
for him but she knew he wasn't there, and Ruth sat down
beside her and said, smiling, 'You have had enough
excitement for one day, and it is coming up to midnight. I
should slip off to bed if I were you.'

'I think that's a marvellous idea,' said Kerry, and she
slunk out with Ruth beside her, across the hall into the
Chinese room. As they walked in Ruth asked, 'Was that
a surprise to you? Had he asked you to marry him
before?'

'No, he hadn't.'

'Well, it was a surprise to us.' Ruth smiled wryly. 'Although of course you did get on very well right away.'

Ruth still believed she had interrupted a lovemaking session so that it was no use telling her, 'I don't love him, I don't even fancy him.'

'I'll tell them you need your rest tonight,' said Ruth, and became suddenly embarrassed. 'Or perhaps I don't tell Adrian that, do I?'

'Tell anybody who asks,' said Kerry hastily, and when Ruth went she slipped a bolt on the door. There was a small bag, packed for an overnight stay, and she carried that into the cloakroom and someone knocked as she washed. Then again just before she switched off the light to climb into bed. She didn't answer either time and in both cases it was a light and hesitant tapping that could have been, she thought, either Adrian or Louise.

They didn't persist, and she lay listening to the noise of the continuing party and trying to will herself into a dreamless sleep. She didn't want to dream. In the morning she needed to wake refreshed and relaxed in mind and body. But it was still night when she woke because it was still dark.

She dug into her handbag beside her bed and came up with a small flat torch, and checked the time on the wristwatch that was also in her bag. Nearly half past two o'clock which was terrific. At least five more hours to go before she could reasonably emerge, and nothing to do except lie here and worry because she wouldn't get to sleep again.

As soon as she had opened her eyes she had thought, the party's over, because she couldn't hear a thing. And then, why didn't I say last night that I'm leaving tomorrow? I let them all believe I might be marrying Adrian. I left him thinking that. And David. I didn't want to hurt Adrian by turning him down publicly, and I wanted to give David a bad time because he'd like to chuck me out of the house by the scruff of the neck and I wanted him to think I could end up as one of the family.

Sparing Adrian's face was some excuse, but she couldn't swear that her main reason for keeping quiet had not been to make David Caradoc suffer. Whether it was kindness or cussedness, she had to come clean this morning, and hope that Adrian would understand that although she had had a wonderful fortnight pretending to be Rosalind she was in fact a girl called Caroline Holland—he didn't even know that—who was not planning on marrying anybody.

Perhaps she should have answered the tapping on the door, then she might have had a chance to talk to Adrian alone. By breakfast time the house would be as busy as a hotel, goodness knows how many more had stayed overnight, and any delay in putting the record straight was going to complicate matters. If she had known which was his room she might have gone there now. That would have been awkward because, inevitably, he would get the wrong idea, but she could have said at once, 'We have to talk.' She might have pushed a letter under the door, but she didn't know which door. All the same a letter was a thought, she could weigh her words in a letter and say what she had to say without being interrupted. She might even leave it for him and clear off back to Wayside early. She had packing to do there. It would be better if she left Penlyn as soon as the last performance ended. Back 'home' she had furniture in store in a friend's barn and since she had moved out of her home she had been a paying guest staying with friends. These were temporary measures until she found a place of her own that would be well away from Penlyn.

She got up and switched on the lights and began to work out in her head what she would write. She would tell him that she had been embarrassed when he had announced that they were marrying because they both knew there was no question of that. He knew it as well as she did, and she was leaving today. She could say, 'Your brother thinks you are out of your mind and even if we were genuinely in love your brother would break it up.'

But she wouldn't mention David, and she wouldn't be able to write a letter at all unless she could find something to write it on. She had her small address-phone book in her bag and a little stubby pencil but she needed a sheet of paper and an envelope she could seal, and she opened drawers, in a black lacquered chest which was full of linen, and another under a side table, but there was no writing-paper there either.

She had seen a bureau in the small parlour, and a davenport desk in the drawing-room, perhaps she could find something in one of them, and she slipped on the white towelling robe that Louise had packed in her overnight bag.

There was no sound when she opened her door, but there was a light burning on the gallery and a wall light down there. The stage settings were in the shadows like a ghostly little theatre, and the rows of chairs, but you could see to pick your way through them.

The staircase loomed immense in this dim light and she stood at the bottom looking up to the spot from which she had fallen. She had been lucky. Her ankle ached, without the support of a shoe, but she was lucky that was all that had happened to her. She would play Rosalind in here for the last time tomorrow, unless the sun was shining again and they could go out into the gardens, and she would come down those stairs very carefully indeed.

A movement caught her eye at the top of the stairs, David Caradoc was coming along the gallery. There was enough light to see him. Too much. She could see him and he could see her. He was still fully dressed and smoking a cigar, and she thought wildly that she might have known he wouldn't need as much rest as normal folk. 'Calling on somebody?' he said.

He thought she was off to Adrian's room. He began to come down the stairs, and he wouldn't trip, she could bank on that. He *couldn't* have been waiting in case, so this had to be a coincidence, and if she told him she was looking for an envelope he would believe that about as much as Ruth believed that Adrian was fastening a pin.

She wanted to run, but she made herself pull back her shoulders and lift her head and keep her voice steady, 'And why are you prowling around at this hour?'

He didn't answer, and it wasn't that late. The party was over now and the house was quiet, and whether he had been working or reading or listening to late music or checking the locks and bolts was no business of hers. It was just unlucky chance that he was crossing the gallery while she was at the bottom of the stairs. When he reached her he said, 'A word with you,' and walked on towards the drawing-room.

She could think of a couple of words she would like to shout after him, but she was sure that if she turned for her own room he would move like lightning to stop her. And while she was in the drawing-room she might find an envelope and before he had time to say anything she would say, 'I want to write a letter. That proposal tonight was a farce and the reason I didn't say so at the time was because you were looking at me as if I were something that had crawled from under a stone.'

He turned on lights as he walked in, and when she followed him he closed the door. 'A private word,' she said, nerves as always making her talk rubbish. 'This could be misinterpreted if anyone disturbs us.'

The curtains had been drawn back. It was dark out there but there was no rain on the window panes so perhaps tomorrow's play would be in the open air again. She had crossed to the window and was looking out and she knew he was just behind her; her heart was pounding and a tiny pulse beat in her throat, which had to be because it was going to be humiliating explaining that there was nothing of any depth between herself and Adrian.

'Before you make any rash promises,' he said, 'you should hear a few facts. I'm sure you're fond of Adrian and he appears to be infatuated with you, and we all know Erica thinks you'd make an ideal daughter. But don't imagine you've stumbled into Camelot or the Forest of Arden.'

She turned. He had put down the cigar on an ashtray and smoke curled up slowly. She could smell it. Or she thought she could. 'I have no idea what you're talking about,' she said.

'Of course you haven't. Look around. What do you see?'

What was she supposed to see? Glasses and plates from the party had been removed although the room was hardly in its usual immaculate condition. He was waiting for a reply and she shrugged, 'I see an elegant room after quite a sedate party.'

He took a step towards her and she drew back, and as he turned her to face the window again she stiffened, pressing her hands together. 'And out there?' he said.

He released her almost as soon as he touched her but she could still feel the pressure of his hands on her shoulders. It was dark out there, with no moon or stars. Virginia creeper fringed the window-panes but she could see nothing beyond. 'Gardens?' she suggested.

'My room, my gardens, look further and my estate.' He moved away from her, sat down and looked at her, and his voice was deep and unhurried. 'I don't mind providing for Erica and Adrian,' he said, 'but I'm damned if I'm taking on another star who didn't make it.'

She wasn't all that surprised. Erica carried on as if she

ruled the roost but it was easy to accept that David
Caradoc was master here. It was no concern of Kerry's;
but it meant that David senior must have disinherited his
wife and one of his sons and that seemed unfair.

She asked, 'How come everything belongs to you? I
thought a wife had a claim on her husband's estate.'

He said drily, 'My grandfather was less than impressed
by Erica. She was half my father's age and had much the
same effect on him you seem to be having on Adrian.
Most of the estate was entailed to me. A few years after
my father died Erica had gone through his settlement, so
I hope you're not counting on the cash. Adrian has many
good qualities but money isn't one of them.'

'What about the Galleries?'

'They're in my name too.' That was hard on Adrian
and she said hotly,

'Well, that's a rotten deal when he does all the work
there.'

'Not entirely,' and although it seemed that way of
course she didn't know for sure. She said,

'Well, I'm sure his pictures sell well.'

'Not often enough,' said David. 'So being Mrs Adrian
Caradoc would not be a cushy number. You'd better
continue to look for a job.'

'You don't think I'm good enough for him.'

He didn't deny it. He got up. 'Now you know the score
before you knock on his door,' and she was aware that
her robe wasn't really covering her. It gaped, and
underneath she was in a skimpy nightshirt. She clutched
it closer and he looked her up and down then drawled,
'I'm sure he'd rise to the occasion, but there would be
very few worldly goods coming with that contract so the
real question is—what's your price?'

She had a quick temper although it was a long time
since it had flamed out of control, but now she acted
without hesitating, scooping the first thing to hand, an

ornament from a table, and hurling it at him. He moved aside and it crashed against the wall, and she asked through gritted teeth, 'Was it valuable?'

'Yes.'

'Was it yours?'

'Yes.'

'Good.' She grabbed her robe together again and made for the door, and her ankle stabbed but she didn't limp. At the door she said, 'Does Madeleine know you copped the lot? I bet she does. I bet her price comes high.'

That gave her the last word because she slammed the door, and almost fell over a row of chairs crossing the hall before she got back into the little Chinese room. She bolted that door although there was no danger of him following her in.

She would have liked to go on smashing. If he owned everything she could start on the vase that might be Ming, that was full of roses Adrian had picked from the garden that was David's. Not that she would. One act of wanton destruction was enough, showing that she had lost control, gone to pieces; and she wondered whether he might imagine that was frustration, because the man who was infatuated with her had not turned out to be rich after all.

She was sorry about that for Adrian's sake. Not for her own, it was nothing to do with her, what had snapped her self-control was David Caradoc presuming she had a price. He thought she had been fooling herself that she was going to live like Erica, and when she told Adrian tomorrow that she wouldn't marry him David would be convinced that he knew why.

There would be no more sleep for her tonight. Her ankle was throbbing and her head was throbbing, and she sat cross-legged on the bed hugging her ankle. She – wished she hadn't gone out there and David hadn't told her about the financial set-up. She wished she hadn't fallen down the stairs because that had hurt her ankle and triggered Adrian's public declaration and she couldn't be feeling angrier or more fed up. She had turned out the lights and now she huddled under the sheets.

His bed, she thought, of course I could never sleep in his bed. The aroma of that cigar was still in her nostrils, masculine and heady. In the darkness she could almost imagine that David Caradoc was in the room, and in the morning she would say to Adrian, 'No thank you. I think I'm going into a convent. I hate men.'

On that loony note she must have fallen asleep because the next thing she knew was Erica smiling down at her and asking, 'Are you awake?'

Kerry was, at once and completely.

'I brought you a cup of tea,' said Erica, and there it was on the bedside table. Kerry's watch was at a quarter to nine and she had to get up and dress and make it clear that she was leaving Penlyn this afternoon. Erica said breathlessly, 'I couldn't be happier,' and she sounded ecstatic; and Kerry thought, this is incredible. I could have a police record or a husband, but because I'm a passable actress she couldn't be happier for me to marry her son.

'Please don't,' she begged. 'I'm sure Adrian didn't mean that last night.'

'I'm sure he did,' Erica contradicted gaily. 'I knew from the first how it was going to be. Would you believe me if I said I had a ring?'

She certainly had, on every finger, and Kerry could well believe thay she had one to give to Adrian's wife. But it wouldn't be Kerry.

She felt stifled. She wanted to open the door and push out Erica and her absurdities. 'I must talk to Adrian,' she said.

'Of course you must.' Erica turned to go. 'He's right,'

she said brightly. 'You *are* Rosalind. It's how I think of
you, too.'

Kerry rushed through washing and dressing, suppress-
ing an urge to start shouting, 'Kerry . . . Caroline . . . not
Rosalind.' David didn't think she was Rosalind. He
thought she was too silly for words, with an eye for the
main chance. But he wasn't investing her with any of
Rosalind's graces, he knew play-acting when he saw it
and one actress in the family was enough.

She gave him that. She could understand that. Up till
yesterday she had loved acting in *As You Like It* but after
this afternoon she was never going to play Rosalind
again.

She packed the overnight bag and wondered if she
should zip it up and go. If she could get out of the house at
half past nine without being stopped. If anybody saw her
it would be David, who had a knack of materialising
where she didn't want him to be, but he wouldn't stop
her. He might even carry her bag as far as the gates. Only
then she would have to walk to Wayside and that
wouldn't do her ankle much good. She drank her tea then
stood before the wall mirror and brushed her hair,
delaying coming out of this room to face the fuss that
would be waiting. She doubted if he would offer to drive
her and she wouldn't get into a car with him, maybe she
was allergic to his aftershave, something about him
brought her out in goose-pimples. She was pig-sick of all
the Caradocs, and when the knock came on the door she
answered it still holding her hairbrush.

Adrian stood there and she scowled at him. 'You
shouldnt have said that last night.'

'I know. May I come in?'

She waved him through with her hairbrush and nearly
hit him with it. She must guard against the Caradocs
bringing out a violent streak in her. But he had laid her
open to a very insulting accusation because he had been

fool enough to tell everybody that they were getting married. Not to mention Erica coming in to measure her for a ring. And although she had let it go last night, when she wasn't thinking too quickly, what with the fall and the sedative and a glass of wine, and of course she hadn't thought he was serious, he had better be explaining this morning that he had been joking. Starting with his brother and his mother because they believed he meant it. And if by chance he had meant it the answer was an abolutely final NO.

She dropped the hairbrush into the open bag and started, 'You——' and Adrian blurted,

'There's something I want to tell you.'

He wasn't listening, he was getting out what he had to say and nothing was gong to stop him. He wasn't looking at her and there was something forlorn in the way he stood, bowed head turned away. 'I'm not a rich man. I don't own any of this.'

She bit back flippancy—so what else is new?— because he looked and sounded so wretched. 'That girl I was engaged to thought I was and I hadn't thought it mattered. Everything's in David's name, but he couldn't be more open-handed so why should it matter?'

He looked at her then with bleak eyes and she said impulsively and gently, 'It shouldn't.'

'It did to her. She married someone else when I told her.' Maybe David had warned her off, but that was cruel and Kerry said warmly,

'Then she wasn't worth bothering about.'

'Money wouldn't matter to you?'

'Money's useful, everybody should have it, but of course it wouldn't.' He reached for her and she said hastily, 'If we were serious, which we are not.'

'I am,' he said, and it was an effort to keep him at arm's length while he was trying to pull her close. 'I've wanted you ever since I first saw you.'

'Rosalind,' she said, 'you've wanted Rosalind.'

'Yes.' He couldn't understand what she meant.

You ask your brother about me, she could have said, he'd soon give you another point of view.

'Don't say no,' Adrian was begging her. 'Just leave it. Think about it. Don't just go away and leave me.'

If she did he might believe it was the money. David assuredly would, and she wished there was some way of letting Adrian down without damaging his pride. With a brother as arrogant and successful as David Caradoc his pride must have taken some knocks over the years. She knew that Adrian's feelings for her were superficial—how could they be anything else when he didn't know the real girl at all?

'Stay a little longer,' he pleaded. 'Another week or two.'

Suddenly he reminded her of Coco, it was the hang-dog look, and she gave a choked gurgle of laughter. And then, because it would be dreadful if he thought she was laughing at him, she had to say, 'Well, maybe, just another week.'

CHAPTER SIX

BEFORE Kerry could stop him Adrian had enfolded her in his arms and she gasped, 'Don't get the wrong idea.' Being crushed against him was suffocating her but it was not quickening her pulses a jot, and she jerked her head back from his chest. 'I could stay on another day or two because I don't have any firm plans but that doesn't mean I want an affair. I don't sleep around. It would mean a serious commitment to me and I don't want that, much less marriage.'

'All right. All right.' He loosed her, looking sulky for a moment, but then he smiled and pleaded, 'Please stay, I won't make a nuisance of myself. Come and have some breakfast.'

In the hall, doors were open, there were sounds of hoovering, and in the breakfast-room—this was the first time Kerry had been in here—Ruth and Gerald and Jenny and Griff were sitting with Erica at a big round table eating breakfast, most of them drinking black coffee.

As Kerry and Adrian walked in the talking stopped and they all looked towards the doorway as if they had been waiting. Last night had been something of a cliffhanger, and now they wanted to hear about the happy ending. Adrian Caradoc's proposal had been very romantic, and very nice for Kerry, he was offering her a wonderful life. All her friends were pleased for her, and David Caradoc was the only one who was not expecting her to greet them this morning, blushing and smiling, hand in hand with Adrian. He knew there was going to be no happy ending.

121

David was there too, behind a newspaper, which he lowered to ask, 'How's the ankle?' and Kerry said,

'Thank you, but it's not quite up to driving all the way back to Stowe yet so I'm staying on for a few more days.' They all thought they knew what that meant, and when she added, 'I'll be leaving next weekend at the latest,' only David believed her.

Mrs Bunbury had almost followed them in with more tea and coffee, and to ask what Kerry wanted for breakfast. 'Just toast, please,' said Kerry, and Mrs Bunbury, her tray piled high with used crockery, paused in the doorway to report,

'One of the Sèvres figures is missing.'

'That's all right,' said David, and Kerry could imagine their faces if he had told them, 'She threw it at me.' She wouldn't have put that past him and she heard herself babbling,

'I'll stay at Wayside if they can put me up.'

'Nonsense,' said Erica and at the same time Adrian said,

'No, you won't.'

'It sounds silly,' said Kerry, sitting down and reaching for a coffee-cup, 'but there's this dog at Wayside I've made friends with.'

'Bring him here,' said Erica promptly.

'I want you to stay here,' said Adrian.

David said nothing and Kerry asked, 'Is it all right with you if I stay until next weekend? I'll try not to get underfoot.'

'And I'll do my best to keep out of your range,' he said gravely and she had a mental picture of him stepping out of the path of the flying Sèvres and bit her lip and when he smiled so did she.

Louise and Rob arrived while several of the Players were examining the open-air theatre and deciding, reluctantly, that their last performance would have to be indoors. Kerry was sitting on the steps of the summer arbour while others stood around, testing the spongy wetness of the grass and looking up into the cloudy sky.

'OK?' Louise asked. 'You'll be all right for this afternoon?' She sat down beside Kerry who said she was fine. 'I wish we could have been out here,' sighed Louise, 'I've got the creeps about those stairs,' and then, 'Look, I'm sorry I went on about him. I didn't realise how it was between you two, I didn't dream he wanted to marry you.' It was easy for her to get enthusiastic about Adrian Caradoc again because she considered him the most eligible man Kerry was ever likely to meet. 'Wow,' she said, 'won't you be rich? Just look at this place. Just imagine living here.'

'Don't let your imagination run away with you,' said Kerry wryly, and Louise stared at her.

'You're never going to play hard to get? Nobody gets an offer like this twice in a lifetime. The young Mrs Caradoc, Mrs Adrian Caradoc,' she made it sound impressive and she said, 'Sounds good.'

'You think so?' said Kerry. If they had been alone she might have told Louise that she never would be answering to 'The young Mrs Caradoc' but by then Rob had joined them on the steps and for the rest of the morning there was always a crowd around.

None of the Players asked Kerry directly if she was marrying Adrian but as soon as they heard she was staying on everybody took that for granted. 'Smashing isn't it?' said Sandra, squeezing her arm. 'Just like a book, isn't it?' and Kerry thought how disappointed they would all be when she did turn up next weekend. She tried to keep things light by smiling now and saying, 'But you don't believe everything you read in books, do you?'

'Yes, I do. Most of the time,' said Sandra.

Erica was taking her plan of a little theatre in the old coach-house seriously. It would be big enough once the clutter was cleared out, and in the Players she had an enthusiastic group who were all for as many little theatres as possible. Gerald began briefing her on planning permission and performing rights and they all trooped around, visualising stage and auditorium and dressing-rooms. Kerry went too, and enjoyed the idea as much as anybody, and hadn't the heart to tell them that Erica, who was talking blithely about builders and carpenters and electricians, was broke. And that the man with the money might consider this too expensive a toy.

Maen Bos was open house to them any time, Erica declared, and they all thought it was her house, and that Kerry would be living here too. And if the coach-house conversion got under way they would all feel that they had a part in that. Today was their last performance and the end of the Flower Festival but the Players all expected to return to Penlyn.

For her final Rosalind, Kerry looked like a princess. She was sitting in the room off the gallery that the girls were using as a dressing-room, wearing the red velvet gown, when Erica came in, carrying a flat box covered with faded blue leather. It was a few minutes to curtain-up, or in this case the moment when Orlando and Adam strolled to the spot at the bottom of the stairs which represented an orchard.

'See what I have,' said Erica, and Ruth and Louise and Jenny and Sandra crowded round to see as she opened the box and laid it on Kerry's knee. The rubies glowed like dark fire, a collar of magnificent stones in an antique setting. It took their breath away so that all any of them could do was gasp.

'You must wear it,' said Erica.

'Me?' Kerry squeaked. 'I daren't.'

But everybody else thought she could. Ruth took off the seed pearl and paste diamond head-dress, pushing the hair back into place, and then she lifted the collar reverently from its box and held it round Kerry's throat. My lord, thought Kerry, it looks more theatrical than the props.

It looked beautiful with the ruby red of the velvet gown, and when Rosalind and Celia made their entrance all the actors spotted it and did a double-take. Most of the audience thought it was part of the costume, Erica and Adrian were smiling; and along the row Madeleine Brenner sat with raised eyebrows and beside her David Caradoc looked thoughtful.

Although she had flashed back with Madeleine's name last night Kerry had hardly given her another thought since the first time she met her, at the dinner-party at the beginning of the festival. There were several of her paintings in the Galleries but she had never been in the Galleries when Kerry was. She hadn't been in the audience before and she was not there last night.

Seeing her now, sitting by David, was quite a shock, as though something you had tried to keep out of your mind had forced a way in. Kerry spoke her first lines automatically and then turned back to Celia and lost herself in Rosalind.

At the end, when she should have walked down the staircase hand in hand with Rob, she took the side with the handrail and came down holding that, and everybody laughed with her because they all knew what had happened yesterday.

At the foot of the stairs she spoke the final epilogue, ending, 'When I make curtsy, bid me farewell,' and curtsied deep, raising her head and meeting, by accident of course, David Caradoc's eyes, and thought for the first time that the words were sad. The play was over and very soon she would be lonely again.

Everybody stood up to clap, and Erica made a speech, thanking the audience and the actors and promising that the Players would be back. While the audience filed out

the Players went for the last time into the little parlour
that had been set aside for them these two weeks. None
of them was in a hurry to go, not even those who would
soon be starting the long drive home. They had put on a
good show and they had enjoyed themselves, and they
were reluctant to break up the party. So for a few minutes
longer they chattered and joked.

Adrian stood by Kerry and when he called her
Rosalind she said, 'Rosalind's taken her bow. From now
on I'm either Kerry, or if you want to be formal,
Caroline,' and he smiled and said, 'You'll always be
Rosalind to me.' So if it bothered her she would have to
make a stand and refuse to answer, but by then
Madeleine reached her.

'It seems I've been missing a lot of excitement,' said
Madeleine. 'How did you come to fall down the stairs?'
and she sounded sorry she had missed it.

'I think these had something to do with that.' Kerry
swished the full skirts of her costume and Madeleine
trilled on,

'And then Adrian proposing to you in front of
everybody. He won't be able to get out of that too easily.
You're a clever little thing, aren't you?' Kerry was several
inches taller than Madeleine who was still managing to
look down her nose at her, drawling, 'And Erica's let you
wear the rubies.' Perhaps it was the rubies she was
looking at as they lay warm and heavy against Kerry's
skin. 'You seem to have two of the Caradocs eating out of
your hand, but you won't get round that one in a hurry,'
and Madeleine inclined her head very slightly in the
direction of the doorway and David.

'Two out of three isn't bad.' Kerry tried to sound
amused and Madeleine's lips curved in a smug little
smirk, her eyes still on David.

'I'll take the odd man out,' she said and Kerry
muttered,

'I'm sure you will,' and moved away.

She had to get out of her costume and then she had to go down to Wayside to arrange to stay on after tomorrow, and she wanted to see Coco again. He would have been waiting to see her yesterday.

She passed David in the doorway and he said, 'You look very splendid.' He meant the rubies, of course, and she hoped he didn't imagine she had designs on them. She said,

'I won't be sorry to hand these back. I wouldn't be wearing them if Erica hadn't insisted.'

There was a glint of laughter in his eyes as if this was a joke she didn't understand and she said so softly that no one else overheard, 'I do hope they were hers to lend. Don't tell me these belong to you too.'

He bowed his head, his lips brushing her hair. 'Oh, they belong to Erica, but don't worry about them. The actors aren't the only phoneys around here. Mind you, not many know that.'

Her eyes widened, and then she smothered a giggle behind a hand, looking into his eyes through her heavy theatrical lashes, and suddenly it was very quiet as though the world held its breath. She blinked and the noise all around rushed back at her but for a moment she had been in a strange and secret place.

Madeleine was there, pink-tipped fingers reaching for David's arm, and Kerry said, 'See you,' and left them to walk across the hall—where they were already clearing away the seating—into the little Chinese room. Others would be changing upstairs, and she needed a breathing space to pull herself together.

She shouldn't have been surprised. She had always known that something odd happened to her when she got too close to him. But just now she had gone deaf and blind to everything except his eyes locked with hers. They had blotted out the rest of the room more completely than any other man could have done by covering her ears and kissing her mouth.

She fumbled with the clasp of the collar and put it down on the dressing-table, and leaned over it, fingertips pressed on the table edge. It looked real, but then she wouldn't know. Come to that, any number of Erica's splendid pieces could be copies. The paintings and furnishings in this house were no reproductions, but they belonged to David and telling her about the rubies might have been to stress that she would gain nothing from Erica if she married Adrian.

He need not have bothered. She would be leaving here very soon, and the Players would never understand why she hadn't married Adrian and for years they would talk about the time she wore the Caradoc rubies.

Erica put her head round the door and asked, 'May I come in?' and did.

'The rubies,' said Kerry.

'Ah yes.' But Erica hardly gave them a glance, which did seem to indicate that they were less valuable than they appeared. She looked at the case in the corner instead, that Kerry hadn't noticed although it was her case and somebody must have brought it up from Wayside.

'You must stay here,' Erica pleaded. 'I need you. Please say you'll stay.' She sounded exactly like Adrian. 'Besides, Mrs Hayle is fully booked and there's a fan waiting to see you.' Before Kerry could speak she had called, 'It's all right. You can let him go,' and Coco came flying into the room, hurtling for Kerry, his tail swishing so that everything within range was at risk.

'Sit,' Kerry howled, but by then he had his paws on her shoulders and she was the one who sat down hard on the side of the bed.

'Isn't he a darling?' cooed Erica.

'He could be a menace,' said Kerry. She had already

put paid to a Sèvres figurine, she wouldn't like Coco to add to the damage, although now he was sitting grinning at her and even his sad eyes looked happy.

'He's a lamb,' Erica declared. 'They said he'd been waiting for you. They said you were the only one he's taken to since he was left with them. Mrs Hayle said she didn't mind at all if he came up here.'

'Thank you,' said Kerry. Erica wanted her own way, Kerry here at Maen Bos, although Kerry suspected that whim would fade at about the same rate as Adrian's infatuation. But it had been kind of her to ask about Coco and to arrange for him to be brought here and Kerry was quite ridiculously pleased to see him.

After she had said her goodbyes to the Players who were leaving this afternoon, and they included Louise and Rob, she took the dog walking round the gardens. He raced around on the lawns that had been the theatre and around the grey-stone building that was David Caradoc's studio.

By the time she had finished changing out of her make-up and costume David and Madeleine had gone and she wondered if they were in here. She could imagine him working and Madeleine sitting watching, talking the same language because they were both artists although there was a world of difference in their creations, and she had a strong urge to walk up and knock on the door. But Coco was haring back into the little wood, so she turned away.

That evening she ate out with Adrian, far enough from Penlyn for them to pass unrecognised in the holiday crowds. They sat at a rough wooden table in the courtyard of a tavern, with Coco curled up at Kerry's feet, and it was like all those other evenings they had spent together, except that tonight Adrian did rather more sighing. 'I do love you, you know,' he told her more than once. 'I do want you.'

'Because you can't have me,' she said, and felt certain that if they had been lovers from their first date he would be cooling off by now. But no way could she imagine him as her lover, although it was easy enough to think of him as a friend.

She would rather have stayed at Wayside. She could have said good night to Adrian there and gone up to her room, but sleeping under the same roof she knew what he was thinking and hoping and long after she was in bed she was half expecting the tap on the door.

It didn't come. She spent the night with only Coco's snores to disturb her, and her own thoughts. She had gone to her room at the same time as Erica and Ruth, leaving Adrian and Gerald talking. Adrian had kissed her good night and when she had drawn back a little to offer no encouragement he had said, sadly and very quietly, 'You're hard,' and she said, just as quietly, 'Didn't you know?' So maybe disillusionment was setting in. Nobody had ever accused Rosalind of being hard.

Neither David nor Madeleine had been downstairs while Kerry was there, but that didn't mean they were not in the house, and it was the thought of them in those rooms upstairs with the connecting doors that kept Kerry awake.

'I'll take the odd man out,' Madeleine had said, and the images running through Kerry's mind devastated her with their unexpectedness and their violence. When she did fall asleep they moved into her dreams and when she woke next morning she struggled up gasping from a cocoon of sheets.

Coco stirred as soon as she moved, instantly alert, and she said, 'Hello' and then sat huddled, remembering some of her dreams, her warm skin burning hotter. She could not imagine Adrian as a lover but last night she had imagined David, with a force of feeling that had faded Madeleine out of the picture and put herself into his arms. She had taken the odd man out and he had taken her, and she had never had dreams like these before.

He had been under her skin from the beginning and some of it was antagonism, but some of it was sexual because he was dangerously attractive. Two weeks as David's Rosalind might have been a different story. It would have been ending about now but that could have been sensational, really something to remember as Louise had said long ago. Of course there had never been a chance, he thought she was funny, not fanciable. Most of the time she amused him and the rest of the time she was a nuisance.

She got out of bed and went into the cloakroom. She looked tousle-haired and heavy-lidded, almost as if she had just risen from a night with a lover, and she grinned wryly because this was funny. Her fancying David Caradoc. Most women would, so it didn't make her unique, but it certainly meant that he need not worry about Adrian. She could have told him, 'Your brother couldn't be safer because I have just realised that you would only have to hold me for longer than a few seconds and I would be putty.' She must neither say that nor show that, and she should be getting away from here as soon as possible.

But three days passed by. By Sunday night all the Players had left but the town was full of holidaymakers and the house was still a hive of activity. Now Erica was immersed in plans for the coach-house and as it was all on paper so far Kerry made notes for her, and typed them out and thought it would be nice if it happened. She went down to the Galleries but there Coco was a hazard. After he sent a model composed of twisted wires flying she got him out and didn't take him back. She had hastily replaced the work, nobody else had seen it go, and hoped it wasn't now bent in all the wrong places.

Coco never left her side, and whether the Hayles

would let him leave Penlyn troubled her. Staying with the Caradocs was one thing but he was their son's dog and they might not feel like disposing of him. She put that out of her mind. It was absurd but the animal had become so important to her that she might even consider buying somewhere not too far away to keep him with her.

Louise phoned on Thursday morning. 'I've been trying to get you,' she said. 'I rang last night and got Erica, didn't she tell you?'

'No.' Erica had probably forgotten. Last night Kerry had been out with Adrian and some of the artists from the Galleries. They all regarded her as Adrian's girl although they seemed to accept the relationship as a casual one.

'Are you well settled in?' Louise wanted to know.

'I'm leaving here at the weekend.'

'I had a feeling you might,' said Louise. 'That's why I was ringing. There's a house going in the High Street.' She described it and gave the price and Kerry knew the property and it sounded a bargain. 'Shall I get the keys,' asked Louise. There could be no harm in that.

'Please,' said Kerry.

She had got up from the breakfast table to take the call on a phone in the hall. Her voice had carried through the open door, because as she replaced the receiver Adrian came into the hall and said, 'You're really going back?'

'Yes.'

'You won't get rid of me like that. It's a small country.'

She didn't think Adrian Caradoc would be following her. Phoning her maybe. But surely not wasting much more time on a girl who had proved so unresponsive, and she said quietly, 'I'll be out of sight, out of mind.'

'"From the east to western Ind, no jewel is like Rosalind",' quoted Adrian with feeling, and David who had strolled out of the breakfast-room just behind him grinned. Kerry saw him and she was finding it hard not

to smile because Adrian was deadly serious and so was
Erica who was there too, wailing, 'You can't leave us, you
can't go,' like someone out of an old melodrama.

David said drily, 'As you've just pointed out, it's a
small country,' and Erica turned on him.

'You promised to do a model of Rosalind. You said if
she stayed you would, and she did stay and even if she
insists on leaving soon there's still time for a sketch. If no
one else wants it I shall hang it in my little theatre. Our
first Rosalind.'

'I want it,' said Adrian. 'I asked for it in the first place.'

They sound like squabbling children, thought Kerry,
and she remembered how scared she had been that
David Caradoc might portray her as he saw her which
would be in a very unflattering light. It could settle
Adrian's infatuation if that was the picture she left
behind, but when David said, 'All right,' she protested.

'How long would it take?'

'Hardly any time,' he said. 'I'll see you at the mine
unless you've anything else planned for this morning.'

This week she had been walking on the downs with
Coco again, taking the old road and looking down on the
ruins, wondering if David was using that building that
had been restored at the end of the row. And now, while
she was hesitating, 'I've nothing planned, but——' he
strode off, and Erica and Adrian started up again.

Erica's voice was the shriller, Adrian just sounded
mournful. He knew Kerry meant what she said, but
Erica would not accept that she was turning down a
chance to help create a little theatre; Kerry thought that
when she finally did drive away Erica would still be
wailing, 'Of course you're not going.'

The good weather had not returned. Kerry was
wearing jeans and a shirt and she went back into her
room to get her denim jacket because cool winds were
blowing over the downs. This was a lovely little room.

She would be sorry to leave it, but the holiday was definitely over.

The roses in the Chinese vase had lasted well, although roses without thorns were not her, and you had to almost bury your face in them to catch a whiff of fragrance because they didn't have much scent either. The full-blown flower she brushed shed a few scarlet petals and she said to Coco, 'You see. Our time's running out. Let's go and find the man who's going to paint our portrait.'

Coco was delighted. The moors were his favourite place. He rushed around as always, chasing things that got away. Kerry's ankle was giving her no trouble now but she avoided the rougher ground and the rabbit holes and walked slowly. She wasn't rushing to reach David Caradoc, and the moment of truth when he sketched her as he saw her. This could be the last time she walked to the old mine on the old road and a faint melancholy settled on her so that her mood matched the grey skies.

She had to think positively. She had come here feeling that nothing mattered much, but while she had been here she had come alive again, and she must not go home and slip back into depression.

The house that Louise had found was a nice little house. Just big enough and cheap enough. She could furnish that with the furniture she had and settle in comfortably. The rooms would seem very small after Maen Bos, but what rooms wouldn't? And all the men she knew or was likely to meet were going to seem dull compared with David Caradoc. That was something she would have to live through. She would, of course, but it wasn't a cheering thought.

Coco raced by, head back, full pelt after a bird that was high in the sky and that vanished into the clouds, leaving him earthbound and gasping.

'You are a *fool*,' Kerry told him, adding ruefully, 'but we have got a lot in common.'

The door was open. If it had not been she might not have gone in after all, because from the time she stood on the hill, looking down into the valley with the ruins of the tin-mine spread out below, she had become more and more nervous. It was like stage-fright, the tightening of her muscles and the butterflies in her stomach. But when she drew near the door he appeared in it and said, 'You're late.'

'I didn't know I was expected to run.' She felt as if she had. She was breathing fast as she followed him into the room.

It was very light, with windows and skylights and stone white-washed walls. There was no sign of any completed work, although there was a portfolio on the big wooden-topped table that must have come from an old-fashioned kitchen. There was a big cupboard reaching from ceiling to floor, two wooden chairs, one armchair, one straightback, and a knee-desk on the table that he must use as a drawing-board.

Coco padded in and around and then sat in the open doorway watching Kerry and she asked, 'Where do you want me?' and thought how silly that sounded when he obviously did not want her at all. Except briefly as a model, and that only because he had been reminded of a reluctant promise.

He pointed to the hardback chair which was set by a window and she sat down, her long legs crossed at the ankles and tucked under. She would have to pretend herself into some role or other, act a part, because she couldn't just sit here defenceless while he stared long and hard at her the way he was doing.

He was sitting at the table, chin in hand, and she wanted to put her own hands in front of her face and hide behind them. She couldn't look straight at him, and she pulled a laughing grimace. 'What do I do now?'

'Sit still,' he said. 'How do you want to look, like

Rosalind?' His voice was deeper than Adrian's, but when he quoted, 'Let no face be kept in mind but the fair of Rosalind,' he gave it just the same intensity that Adrian had this morning, but he grinned and so did Kerry.

'No thanks,' she said promptly. 'I've had enough of Rosalind.'

'Haven't we all?' He began to sketch and there was quiet for a few minutes. Coco had realised they were staying and was now lying down facing outdoors, and she would have liked to jump up and run just as much as he would. What was she doing here anyway? She didn't want a sketch of herself by the great David Caradoc. Anyhow she wouldn't be getting it, and she was pretty sure that when they saw it neither Erica nor Adrian would like it.

'I've never had my portrait done before,' she said.

'It's painless.'

'So you say. Sitting here I feel like those sets of Russian wooden dolls that you take apart and they get smaller and smaller and finish up about this big.' She held finger and thumb a fraction apart, and went on chattering because once she had started it was hard to stop. 'That one's solid but hardly worth the trouble.'

He had to hear her but he went on with what he was doing and she thought, this is a lightning sketch like the seaside artists do. Ten minutes and you're through, and why couldn't he have asked me to sit still for ten minutes in Maen Bos?

'You're leaving this weekend?' he said.

'Promise,' she said.

'Why didn't you leave with the others? Someone would have given you a lift and I'm sure somebody could have driven your car back.'

She sat straighter. 'Sure they could, only I didn't feel like leaving at the time. You should have said you minded me moving into your house. Wayside might have been fully booked but I could have got lodgings somewhere else. You must bill me.'

'Don't be ridiculous,' he said. 'But you had made up your mind not to marry Adrian. You're no longer having an affair with him.' She tried to say, 'I never was,' but he went on, 'You're not sleeping with him?'

'How would you know?'

'Because he's looking so miserable.' These last few days had not made Adrian happy. He was getting sulkier and although he would protest when she left it wouldn't break him up. But like everybody else David Caradoc thought they had been lovers and she drawled, 'Maybe that's because our mad passionate lovemaking is starting to bore him and he's getting tired of me.'

'No.' He sounded definite about that. 'But I still can't work out why you stayed,' and she told him the truth.

'I thought I'd let him down gently. Once I stopped playing Rosalind he'd see I'm pretty ordinary. I think it's working. When I do leave here I don't think he's going to follow me. Besides——'

She wondered what he was making of her face. He was getting something down in swift decisive lines, definitely a lightning sketch so it shouldn't be long before she could get out of here. 'Besides what?' he queried and she had to think to remember.

'Oh, well, he told me he'd got no money. The morning after you did, before I had time to open my mouth, and that was why the last girl walked out on him, so I couldn't turn round and go right away.'

'Very considerate.'

'What was she like?' She wasn't really curious, but it was something to say.

'Katie?' He looked up and down, transferring what he was seeing on to the white sheet of cartridge paper. 'Pretty. Not over-bright.'

That's what you think of me, she thought, not over-bright. But she said nothing because that might influence him slightly and she didn't want to come out looking too stupid. He went on, 'It was even betting between Adrian and another man and cash could have decided it.'

'Did you tell her too?' He shook his head. 'Just me you warned off?'

'Yes.'

She mimicked his sardonic, 'Very considerate,' and there was another silence while neither spoke and she looked around, moving her eyes, trying to keep her head still. Then she said, 'It's emptier than I expected. Don't you work much in here?'

'On ideas. Most of the physical work I do in the studio. It's quiet out here.'

'It wasn't always,' she mused. Through the open door there was nothing to see but moorland. If she had turned and looked through the window she would have seen a tall chimney and the ruins of an engine-room but from where she sat there was no sign left of the Caradoc mine, and yet once—— 'What did it look like?' she asked. 'Do you know?' and he described how it was when over two hundred men had laboured there.

And women too, the bal-maidens who worked in the picking sheds, hammering the tin ore from the rock brought up from the mine. They were not allowed below ground which would have been bad luck, although there couldn't have been much good luck in breaking rocks in all weathers in an open-sided wooden shed.

The mine had closed down a hundred years ago. 'My father had the idea of turning it into a tourist attraction,' said David. 'He had this row of buildings restored. This used to be the counting-house, and farther along were storerooms and a smith's shop. That was getting on for twenty years ago. I kept this room going. He had a lot of work done underground too, but it's impossible to keep it safe, it's a death-trap down there. It was a hopeless project.'

'Was that his idea or Erica's?'

He laughed. 'I never knew. I was away at school when it was launched. But now you mention it Erica could have seen herself as queen of the bal-maidens. So long as the weather was good and the hammer was a theatrical prop.'

'And now she wants to build a theatre.' She was relaxed now, the tension had gone. They were joking and she enjoyed listening to his deep sexy voice. 'Pity about the rubies,' she said. 'They could have financed it. Were they ever genuine, did she sort of do a swap?'

'She sort of did,' he said. 'And if you're going to ask why I didn't stop her I can assure you I have enough trouble stopping her replacing the pictures with some very good copies.'

'Are they her pictures?'

'No, but that wouldn't stop her.'

Coco shot out of the doorway like a greyhound released from the trap, and Kerry turned her head to watch him through the window. 'I hope it's a rabbit,' she said. 'He never catches them but if it should turn on him rabbits don't have very sharp teeth, do they? Coco,' she called, and then she was on her feet, running out of the building, calling louder, until in the end it was almost a scream as the dog wriggled under the boards that fronted a small hillock.

It had to be an old shaft-head and they could drop right down to incredible depths. She gave a great tearless sob of terror and still screaming '*Coco*' fell on her knees and began to tear at the earth and undergrowth under the boards.

'Keep calling him,' said David.

'Is it a sheer drop?'

'No.' But he didn't say it was all right. She crouched

over the small hole through which the dog had squirmed, cupping her mouth, and shouting into the darkness, and then she heard the sound of wood splintering and looked up to see David levering a board away with a chisel. She still couldn't see in and called 'Coco' again and this time her voice echoed and when the echoes died there was a rustling sound like the wind in the trees.

Then another board gave way and he put a hand on her shoulder. 'Stay here, keep calling.' He picked up a torch and climbed through the splintered wood and she followed right behind him.

She had never known such blackness. The little light filtering in showed nothing and he said, 'Go back,' in a voice that brooked no argument, and she wasn't arguing but she was going after Coco. She called him again, taking a step and starting to slip. It was gravelly underfoot, and a light came on and David grabbed her. 'You're not too good on stairs, are you?' he said.

'Stairs?' The torch beam showed her a steep decline going down and down, although when she moved her foot again—he was still holding her arm—she could feel a hard edge.

'In the old days it was a ladder,' he said. 'My father put in steps.' He shone the torch down. The dog would have slithered and rolled to the bottom, that was the noise she had heard, shifting shale, but Coco was making no sound now and she had to get to him. There was a wooden handrail fixed to the rock-side. She reached for it and began a slow descent, calling, 'It's all right, you're going to be all right. Good boy, don't be frightened.'

She was frightened. Even with the torchlight and with the man who always seemed to be a step ahead this was a hellish place. Wild horses wouldn't have dragged her down there but she was probably the only one who could stop that clown of a dog panicking and getting buried alive. If he hadn't broken his neck already, and she wouldn't think about that. She would take one step at a time, down the iron stairs that were covered with earth and gravel.

When she stood at the bottom she realised that David still held her arm and that he had been supporting her and she said, 'Thank you,' and it sounded as if he had helped her off a bus or opened a door for her. But she had to be very controlled because she couldn't see Coco and it was wet and dank down here with the black tunnels and crevices, and the dog must have run or crawled into this labyrinth that could stretch for miles.

The beam of the torch showed glistening rock and dripping water and she remembered that the mines flooded and knew that he could drown in the darkness unless she reached him or her voice stopped him. David was flashing the torch down the main tunnel and she shouted, 'Coco, where are you? He'll hear me,' she said. 'He'll bark, you see,'

They listened and the sounds were soft and strange, creakings and sighings, but no dog barked. 'I can't leave him,' she said.

'Will you stay here? I know the workings, I'll find him.'

She lied, 'I'm scared of the dark, I can't be left alone,' and tried to smile, and pleaded, 'If he's hurt and scared he might run from you but he'd come to me.'

'All right. Go on talking to him.' He stepped ahead of her between timber props and over cables probably dating from David Caradoc senior's plan to open the mine. The torchlight cast grotesque shadows, revealing at every turn deep black chasms so that David's earlier words—'It's a death-trap down there'—were never out of her mind.

Coco was trapped somewhere and so might they be, even if David did know the plan of the place. But she bit her lip and never asked, 'You do know the way out?' as they stumbled down the slimy passages where the air was hot and stagnant, climbing over rocks and debris. An animal could be anywhere. There were cracks and burrows in the rock and tunnels hardly high enough to crawl along. Passages almost blocked by rock falls. He could be where they could neither see him nor reach him. If they didn't find him she would come back with a stronger light and search every inch, but if she left here today without him she would not deceive herself that she would find him alive.

She called and they listened and there was never complete silence. Once there was even faint tapping, and she turned wide eyes to David, 'What's that?'

'The tinners had a name for it,' he said. 'The knackers. I'll tell you about them some time.'

'I think I'd rather you didn't tell me while we're down here,' and she heard her own forced laughter. But there was never an answering bark and soon she would have to admit that Coco was lost. She shouldn't be asking anyone else to endanger themselves like this because if the rock didn't get you the gas probably would. The air was fetid. It was not only distress that was making her head ache. She would have to give up and go back. If only she could stop feeling that in just another minute she would find the poor creature who had thought he was safe so long as she was around.

'Beyond this it's flooded,' said David. They were in a passage where she walked unsteadily with her head ducked and he was practically bent double, and when he held the torch still she could see the barrier of rocks at the end of it.

'August 1842,' he said, 'they struck a subterranean river, everything below this level began to flood. Pumps and drainage couldn't keep pace and it was closed down a few months later. About forty years before the rest.'

She looked at the rocks, glistening wet, and could

imagine the deep black waters beyond. Through a gap she shouted 'Coco' and her voice cracked because he was never going to hear her, and a howl like a banshee's answered sending her reeling back against David, gasping, 'You heard that? What was it? Do you think . . .?'

'I'll tell you the legend of the hairless hound some time,' he said. 'But that one I think is yours.'

CHAPTER SEVEN

KERRY screamed 'Coco' again and the howling increased. Whatever it was was desperate to get out, and of course it was Coco although she was in such a state that she almost believed in a phantom hairless hound. Her fingers scraped against a rock in the barrier and David said, 'Steady, don't bring them down. Here, hold the torch.'

There was cement between some of the rocks but some were loosely packed and he eased several out and when there was room enough she said, 'Let me go.'

'Just hold the torch.' He barred her way and grunted with the effort of hauling down the barrier until there was space for him to get through himself. Again she was right behind him, and waiting for them was a lake, black as pitch, moving sluggishly against the rock walls. For a little way there was a slope of gritty earth, black waters and black beach like something out of a nightmare, and she stood, a hand clapped over her mouth, her head spinning.

David moved the torch, sending an eerie glow over the water, skimming the rock face, and two green eyes glowed and Coco gave out another full-throated howl and Kerry could have burst into tears. The dog had found a footing over there. He crouched in a niche and he could go no further and she had found him and she was happier than if she had found a diamond the size of her fist.

'Shut up, you howling idiot,' she screeched. 'It's bad enough down here without you kicking up a din like the planet of the damned. Come *back*, you stupid animal.'

The howls faded into a whimper but the dog didn't

move, and her tone changed too and became pleading. 'Come on, it's all right, come on now.' But he never moved a muscle and she stepped towards the water's edge and David caught her elbow, demanding,

'Where do you think you're going?'

'Getting him.' There was no way round.

'You're not wading through that,' he said. 'It's deep. Try calling him again.'

The dog could be hurt or just so scared that he was literally paralysed and she talked on, soothing, cajoling, and Coco went on whimpering but showed no sign of jumping from his ledge back into the water.

David took off his shoes and his shirt and was stripping off his trousers and she asked stupidly, 'What are you doing?'

'I was thinking of raping you,' he said impatiently. 'What do you think I'm doing? Fetching your damned dog.'

She said no but he took no notice, and she held the torch in both hands and even then she couldn't keep it steady. In the darkness this seemed a great stretch of water and he had said it was deep but there were probably more rocks down there, just under the surface maybe. God knows what was down there. Underwater currents, prehistoric monsters. This was a nightmare she could be dreaming for the rest of her life.

She was running up and down on the little slope of mud and clay and as he reached the shelf where Coco lay her foot slipped and she went down on her knees and stayed there. She saw him reach up and pull the dog towards him, and he called, 'He's all right, just scared,' but she couldn't answer for chattering teeth.

He had Coco in the water and the dog clung to him like a monkey, and he came back with it perched on his shoulders gibbering with cold and fear. On the clay soil it clawed its way to Kerry and she put down the torch very carefully and hugged the squirming creature, burying her face in its wet fur.

David said, 'He's all right. Here,' he threw his shirt towards her. 'Rub him down.' She wrapped him and rubbed him and tears were streaming down her face and when he had shoes and trousers on again the man went down on his heels beside her and said, 'Are those the real thing?' touching her cheek. He was smiling but the eyes she turned towards him were brimming and her voice rose hysterically.

'I'm not acting and you don't know the half of it. I can't stand up. I have done for my ankle this time.' It hurt like red-hot knives. The thought of scrambling over rocks and walking those craggy uneven tunnels made sweat stand out on her forehead. She said wildly, 'I'll have to stay here. If I could have some pain-killers maybe I could get along, but like this I can't move.'

She would have to wait in the darkness and it would be a long time before anybody could get back to her, but she must not get hysterical although the pain was excruciating. She sobbed, 'Perhaps you could leave me somewhere not quite so horrific, a bit drier,' because he would have to take the torch to find his own way out, but she did not think she could sit here, hurting so, beside this sinister black sea.

'Another fine mess,' he said, and he drew her close to him as gently as if he were holding a child, assuring her, 'There's no question of your being left down here,' and for a moment she huddled against him, drawing strength and comfort in the same way that Coco had when she had cuddled him.

Her tears mingled with the gritty wetness of his skin, and she sneezed and tried to smile. 'Not even with Coco?'

'Especially not with Coco, who seems to be more accident-prone than you are,' he said, and that made her giggle. She clenched her teeth and swore to herself that if he would help her she wouldn't make a fuss if it killed her. It would hurt but if she was left in the dark down here she could very easily crack up.

When he lifted her she put no weight at all on her injured foot and she started to babble, 'I'm not that light, I'm going to feel heavy, can you manage me?'

'When necessary,' he said, 'every time.' And he was smiling but she was suddenly sure that he would get her out of the mine just as he would succeed in anything he put his mind to. So long as she clung to him she would come into daylight.

He gave her the torch. He used both his hands getting her along, lifting her, easing her through the gap in the rocks, supporting and carrying her down the passages. Each jolt stabbed her ankle but she bit hard on her under lip. She would have been lost down here. She was undecided at the first turning, asking, 'Which way?' but he took the right-hand fork without hesitation and it was the way they had come. 'You do know,' she said.

'Yes.' He was carrying her here, slowly, it was rough underfoot. 'But it isn't a place for strolling in, I must have the entrance bricked up. There've been more rockfalls since I was down here.'

Coco was padding and panting alongside them, close as a shadow, and she said, 'I couldn't leave him. He's been abandoned once and I know how it feels.'

'Have you been abandoned?'

She had one arm round his neck and she held the torch in the other, keeping the beam on the obstacles in their path, and she found herself telling him. It helped her forget the pain, and she wanted him to understand. 'My father was stationed abroad,' she said. 'My mother died when I was a baby and it felt like being abandoned because as long as I could remember I was at boarding-school. Holidays I usually stayed with friends. I had no family so I had no roots and no real security. Maybe that's why I can act, I've always been good at pretending. It wasn't my father's fault of course, and he was demobbed and opened a driving-school the year I finished school, and I worked there and we had a home.'

She had spoken soft and fast, her face turned away from him, looking ahead down the passage, although she was seeing another scene.

'And now you don't have a home,' he said. 'Has he gone away again?'

'Not long ago. A long way away. He died.' She hadn't said that since she came here, she had almost pretended it hadn't happened.

'I'm sorry,' said David.

'So that's why I couldn't leave Coco. There was no warning, you see. One moment everything seemed fine, everything was safe, and the next,' she stared into a gorge that the torchlight left in shadow, 'it was like falling into a black hole. Like Coco did. So I had to find him because we've got a lot in common.' She looked at David then and managed to smile. 'And we're both accident-prone.'

'Some day some man is going to have his hands full with the pair of you,' he said, and she knew whose hands she wanted to reach for and hold for the rest of her life. She gulped at that because he was holding her now, because she couldn't walk, just as he would have carried Coco if the dog had been injured. There was nothing lover-like about it. He was gentle enough now, but once he had safely delivered her he would be as tough as old boots again.

Her fingers touched the scarline on his shoulder blade and she traced it a little way and asked, 'How did this happen?'

'Down here,' he said. 'A rock fall. I was modelling the Tin Miner at the time and I used to come down and commune. I wore a tin hat but I got this.' The flickering torchlight was rather like the light from the candles that the miners had worked with and with his powerful build, stripped to the waist and streaked with mud and clay, David Caradoc could have passed she thought for one of those men. That glancing rock must have laid open the skin horribly. If he had not worn a protective hat he could have been killed, and she gulped again, and wanted to say, 'Don't come down here again, promise me.'

But he would promise her nothing, why should he? So instead she said brightly, 'You don't think the old ghosts might have been warning you off?' and he grinned with a flash of white teeth against the grime of his face.

'I rather hoped they were making me a blood brother. Most of them must have carried scars.'

'You were on your own? You didn't have a girl with you? You said it was bad luck if a woman went down the mine, and I believe you because look what it's done to me. But maybe that was why the rock fell.'

'I was alone,' he said, and it was silly to be pleased about that when it was probably years ago and she heard herself asking,

'How long have you known Madeleine?'

'A fair while,' he said and she wondered, what do you call a fair while for a love affair? Louise had been told that David Caradoc was 'never short of female company but they make the running, not him', and he considered Madeleine Brenner was none of Kerry's business. He was right. She could easily start envying Madeleine, and that would be insane. It would irritate David, and how Madeleine would enjoy it.

By now they were back at the bottom of the slippery steps. High up you could see the gap where the boards had been levered away, and it was a long climb when you couldn't even stand unaided. Although she had been carried and supported all the way here she was more exhausted than she would have been if she had been able to get along on her own. The pain from her ankle had stiffened her muscles and, after that moment or two when she had relaxed against him, whimpering like Coco, his continuing touch had kept her tense.

'I could sleep for a week,' she said. 'I can't remember ever feeling so weary. If you don't count the tranquilliser you gave me after I tripped on the stairs.'

'I'll throw you down a sleeping bag,' he said, 'and you can doss down here.'

He was joking, she hoped, and she said, 'Sorry. I've been carried. You must be shattered.'

'Must I?' He wasn't. He was steady as a rock, still holding her, steadier than some of the rocks. 'Hang on,' he said, and took the handrail, admitting, 'I'm not sure about this, but if we go slowly we'll be all right.'

'Maybe I could crawl up.'

But he was getting up and she kept one arm around his neck showing each step with the torch. Coco had scrabbled a little way, when he struck loose earth and went slithering down and startled howling again.

'You run,' David threatened, 'and you're on your own.' But Coco had done with running. He stayed where he was, his piercing cries rising and echoing as though a pack of wolves were down below baying at the moon.

Kerry did crawl through the gap. She rolled out on to the grass and looked back and up to David to plead, 'You will fetch him, won't you?'

'Don't tempt me,' he said, and she called idiotically, 'Be careful,' and then thought she should have stayed at the top, holding the torch, but when she dragged herself back and stuck her head through, the moving light was a long way down. She almost called 'Coco' but that might make the dog wriggle out of the man's hold. So there was nothing she could do, except watch the light going down and down.

Her leg was aching badly and she drew back to look at

it. It was swollen, bulging over the top of her shoe and stretching the bottom of her muddy jeans. She eased off her slip-on pump, and looked at the bruised foot. She knew, without trying, that she couldn't stand on it, and that she would have to wait here like a dumped sack, and her helplessness almost overwhelmed her.

It had started to rain while they were underground, soft and soaking, and she lay sprawled, propped up against the little hillock. David would be all right. He would get down the slope and up again with Coco, and then he would get her back to the house, but all this had to reinforce what he had thought from the beginning, that she was trouble. She didn't want to be trouble. She wanted to be strong and beautiul and she wanted him to make love to her. She must look horrible. She felt as battered and bruised as her foot and she turned her face up to the rain because she felt filthy too.

Coco slunk out of the gap and crawled to her, ears down, tail beween his legs, so dirty that the white fur was grey and only his rolling eyes showed pure white. He had had the fright of his life and David said, 'How was that for a rabbit hole then?'

'Thank the nice gentleman,' said Kerry. 'He didn't enjoy going down there after you. It's turned his hair a funny colour as well.' She thought of the bathroom in Maen Bos that David shared with Madeleine, and was riven with jealousy and said brightly, 'I can't make up my mind whether I'd rather be under cover in the counting-room and filthy or lying out in the rain getting washed and pneumonia.'

He smiled but as he picked her up he said gently, 'You're all right now,' as she had to Coco, and she knew he thought she was still jittery even though the danger was over. And so she was, but this was a different danger that could hurt more than a throbbing ankle. She wanted him to kiss her as he carried her. Her hands were clasped loosely around his neck, his face was just above hers. Just a little pressure, her fingers in his hair, would draw his face down so that her lips could brush his mouth. Lightly again, and then she could smile and say, 'That's a thank-you from both of us. It was kind of you to save Coco. It was very friendly.'

He would take a kiss as a friendly gesture, but the thought of it made something shake inside her and she knew that for once she would not have been able to pretend. If they kissed he would know she was starving for him.

So instead she shut her mouth and her eyes until he stepped on to the flagstones of the old counting-room. Then she opened her eyes, and mouth because the doors of the big cupboards were wide and there was a kettle and a small camping-stove and a jar of instant coffee and she said, 'I could murder a strong black coffee. It's a bit much to ask after you've just been swimming, but is there any water?'

'Yes,' he said, and he perched her on the edge of the big working-table, where she kept the injured foot swinging, and took a roll of bedding that turned out to be a thick sleeping-bag out of the cupboard. Then he lifted her on to the sleeping-bag, where she sat, propped up against the wall. 'Get this down,' he said, and she had half a tumbler of whisky in her hand, and she started to babble about all home comforts until she realised that her hands were still shaking so badly that the whisky was nearly slopping out of the glass.

She swallowed some of it. It stung her lip and burned her throat but it was the nearest thing to an anaesthetic she was going to get for a long while. She didn't know which was worse, the throbbing ankle or this emptiness inside her. But as she watched him filling the kettle from a plastic container, lighting the stove, she yearned to get him closer as if he could ease her ankle and that other ache that had settled round her heart.

When he did come over to her she held her breath, but it was only her injury he was interested in. Her jeans were thick with mud where she had fallen down by the water's edge and he eased them slowly over the swollen foot, and she wasn't fooling herself that this meant a thing to him but getting the patient comfortable. She rolled inside the sleeping-bag and finished the whisky and said, 'Thank you very much' to a mug of black coffee.

Coco was sound asleep on the bottom of the sleeping-bag and David said, 'I'll be as quick as I can. I'll fetch the Range Rover and we'll get you back.'

'Stay for coffee,' she pleaded. 'You must need a drink. Is there any more whisky?'

'Do you want any more?'

'Lord, no. But I want you to have something. *Please.*' Once he went the togetherness and intimacy of this crazy adventure were over.

'All right,' he said. He made another instant coffee and she sat up, sipping hers, watching him. Then she asked, 'What are the knackers?'

He sat down again at the table, the coffee-mug at his elbow, slipped the drawing he had made of her into a drawer and put another sheet of cartridge paper on the sketch board. 'Little men who lived underground before the miners came,' he said. 'The sound of their tapping always meant trouble. They are about two feet tall with shaggy red hair, big heads and bandy legs.'

He was sketching as he spoke and she laughed, 'They've got the mine to themselves now. Are there any lady-knackers?'

'Must be but none have been spotted. Shy, maybe.'

'If they've got big heads and bandy legs I can understand that. And what about the hairless hound?'

'He wanders around.'

'Perhaps he was what Coco chased into the mine.'

'He doesn't come up. He's strictly a below-ground hound-dog.'

The door was a little ajar, she could see the rain and she thought, I wish he would shut the door and stay here. The whisky had dulled the pain and even on the cold floor, the sleeping-bag was cosy. She wished he would go on sketching and talking, telling her the old superstitions of the mines like a bedtime story. There was probably a paraffin lamp in that cupboard where there seemed to be all manner of useful things. When night fell she would like to light a lamp and have David come and lie beside her and hold her in his arms, and tell her he hadn't minded the trouble she had caused because he liked having her around, and one good thing about her latest mishap was that she couldn't go away next weekend now.

She wondered how he would react when he thought about that and knew he would not be pleased. She was. She didn't want to leave. She hadn't for quite a while, and that was because of David. She sat, huddled in the sleeping-bag, thinking back to how violently he had entered her life in the darkness of that first night. And how, in the past weeks, everything she did, all her thoughts and dreams, seemed to come back to him as if he were at the centre of her world.

She sighed because the woman who mattered to him was Madeleine, and that was a terrible waste.

'I'll be back soon,' he said, he thought she was sighing because her foot was hurting and she tried to say, 'I'm fine,' but he brought the sheet of paper to her and said, 'I'll lock the door.'

'I promise to stay put.'

'And push the key underneath. If you get bored you can start hopping.'

'Coco isn't up to it.' Coco squinted through slitted eyes and sank back into deep slumber. 'We'll wait for the taxi,' she said, and he smiled and took the empty coffee-mug from her, looking down at her for a moment and she willed him to kiss her. But instead he said, 'I'll be back within the half-hour.'

'Will you take my jacket?'

'I'm all right.' He went, closing and locking the door, and she watched the key appear on the flagstone just inside. He could have knotted her denim jacket over his shoulders, he certainly couldn't have got arms and shoulders into it but it was raining and he was naked to the waist.

'The man hasn't even got a shirt to his back, thanks to you,' she told Coco. 'It would have served you right if the hairless hound had got you,' and she turned to the big sheet of paper lying beside her and started giggling because they were irresistible: a grinning gnome wielding a tiny hammer; a girl-gnome, making eyes through a wild shock of hair; and a hairless dog that managed to look like Coco, perched on a rock, smiling at them.

She would keep it for ever. The picture of herself she didn't much want to see. If she had she could have worked her way over to the drawer in the table, but she would see that soon enough. This sketch would bring back the good memories. It had been grim down the mine and she was still in pain and likely to be for ages. But when she looked at the gnomes and the hound she would always remember how David Caradoc had carried her and made her comfortable and safe and kept her smiling. She would remember how lovely it was to have him looking after her.

The exhaustion was coming back, and she stretched to put the sketch on the straightbacked chair—she didn't want Coco making a bed on it—then she pulled the sleeping-bag up around her and closed her eyes. Nobody would be sending her away for a few more days, and while she was at Maen Bos she would see David and maybe before long he would realise that he might miss her if she went. If he would only kiss me, she thought, as she fell asleep, then he would know.

She woke when he touched her cheek and at the same time Coco barked sleepily. It was warm in the sleeping-bag and she didn't want to move. Her ankle would throb as soon as she shifted and she wished she could say, 'I'm sure I shouldn't be jolted back to civilisation. Stay with me till morning.'

He was wearing a grey roll-neck sweater but his hair was still matted with mud and obviously he had wasted no time. She smiled and said, 'How nice to see you. What happens to me now?'

'Take these.' He gave her two Panadols with a little water. The key was still on the floor by the door so he must have let himself in with another, and then poured water into the glass before he came across to where she and Coco lay. She hadn't heard him and neither had Coco. She said,

'You'd make a good burglar. You've got a quiet way with you.'

'You think so?'

David Caradoc's quietness was the confidence of inner strength. When he talked people listened, so he would never need to shout. Just as he would never need to make a noise to attract attention when he entered a room. He had an inborn natural force. 'You didn't wake me,' she said. 'Nor my guard dog.'

'Because you and your guard dog are knackered.'

'Absolutely. Can you get us back?'

'Of course.'

She unzipped the sleeping-bag and grimaced at her foot, which was pink and puffy and tender, and again he carried her, this time setting her into the back seat of the Range Rover. Coco jumped in too and as they took the hill and the vehicle juddered she bit her lip again and said, 'Thank you for looking after us.'

He chuckled, 'You must have been a very well-mannered child,' and she laughed too because her voice had sounded wistful and young. She supposed she was a fairly polite child. Holidays she was always thanking somebody for having her.

The mud was stiff on his hair and she longed to reach over and try to brush it away. Just to touch him. If you would care to have me I think I would say thank you, she thought, and she bit her lip again, and sat for the rest of the way with her arms folded tightly because although he drove slowly and carefully it was an uncomfortable trip.

Things didn't get better right away either. Erica was waiting for them at the gates that led to the moors from Maen Bos, and tripped along beside the car registering concern in her usual theatrical fashion. As soon as they stopped and the car door was opened she shrilled, 'An accident in the mine,' and it sounded just like a line from a play.

'I turned my ankle again,' said Kerry. 'That's all.'

Coco, matted and filthy, jumped out, and Erica, who was wearing a cream silk suit and a flowing scarf, backed away. David got out of the driver's seat and another man got in. Kerry recognised him as one of the gardeners, and as Erica climbed in too she asked, 'Where are you going?'

'You need an X-ray on that,' said David.

She supposed so. Her weak ankle had never hurt this badly before. She wouldn't be surprised if she had broken every bone in her foot. She wished that David could have gone with her but the way he looked no hospital would want him over the threshold, any more than Coco, and she grinned and said, 'You want to get cleaned up. You look as if you've had a rough day.'

He looked down at her as she lay, barelegged and barefoot. 'Not as rough as yours. I only lost my shirt.'

She had lost her jeans and her briefs were minuscule. She gasped, 'Please could I have a skirt?' and Mrs

Bunburry bustled off to fetch one and David picked up Coco.

'We'll both get cleaned up,' he said, and to Erica, 'She's very shaken and she doesn't want you chattering away.'

Erica nodded and patted Kerry's hand and hardly said another word. Kerry was surprised that she could be so biddable, and grateful too because her own head was aching. The fear and the foul air she had breathed underground and the pain of her ankle and possibly the whisky were a nauseous combination, and she travelled the ten miles or so with her eyes shut and her stomach heaving.

The hospital looked like a big old country house. They were waiting for her and she was helped into a wheelchair and taken into the X-ray room. No broken bones—this time she was surprised to hear it—but a badly torn ligament, and again the crêpe bandaging. She was to take two pain-killers before every four hours and to lie up for a couple of days. After that she might be able to put her foot down to the ground although she would not be able to flex it and she would be hobbling with a stick for anything up to a month.

She was given the first two pain-killers before they got her back into the car and Erica, who had been chatting animatedly with all the staff, said, 'Hush, dear,' when Kerry tried to say how sorry she was to be causing all this bother.

Kerry *was* sorry. She would have left on Saturday but she would not have bought that house in Stowe. She would have come back and found somewhere here, maybe using Coco as an excuse, finding some reason for living in Penlyn that was not Adrian because she was hooked on David. She would have realised that as soon as she was away from him because the excitement would have gone out of everything.

But she hadn't wanted to be a burden. The Caradocs were not running a nursing home and she could not spend the next four weeks lolling around Maen Bos expecting to be waited on.

She would have to plan, but right now the little Chinese room with the bed with the cool sheets was a haven. She could lie up in there for the two days the doctor had ordered and then she could move into lodgings and nurse her wretched foot back to health.

She said, 'You're being very kind, you must think I'm the clumsiest woman you've ever met,' and Erica smiled her brightest smile and said,

'I knew you couldn't just go away. I've told you all along, it's fate, you and Adrian.'

'And David and Madeleine?' Kerry asked, before she could stop it, and Erica said,

'Perhaps.'

The car was stopping; they were back at Maen Bos, and the driver got out. Erica said, 'We could make a big production of a double wedding,' and Kerry laughed because that was ridiculous, a sick joke, and if she had not laughed she might have told Erica that she was out of her tiny mind.

But it was Kerry's fault for mentioning Madeleine, not Erica's fault at all. And David was there, cleaned up, asking 'Well?' as he opened the car door. Erica made her report over Kerry's mumblings of, 'I'm so sorry but I have to go to bed.'

'Right,' said David, and he got her out and carried her into the house. Coco, sleek and damp after a bath, had joined them, and Mrs Bunbury was in the procession that trooped to the Chinese room, where David put Kerry down on the bed and then stepped back, washing his hands of her. At least that was how it seemed to her. He had, she thought, the relieved look of a man who has done all he needs to do.

'We'll get you comfortable now,' said Mrs Bunbury and Kerry said thank you and watched, with a sinking heart, as David walked out of the room. Goodness knows she could hardly have expected him to stay but she hated to see him go. She almost called, 'You'll come back? I'll see you later?' as he closed the door. She would see him later of course, he lived here, and she was acting like a child wanting his promise. And she had to stop biting her lip, because that was puffy and painful too.

With a little help she managed to wash her face and hands and get out of her soiled clothes into a nightdress. She didn't feel ill if she kept her leg still when she lay in bed, propped up by pillows. She asked, 'Is there anything I can do? Anything I could take down and type out later?' but Erica was not having that. Kerry was to take things quietly for the rest of this day at least. The door would be left ajar, and if she needed anything she was to ring the little brass bell with a dragon coiled round it that they put on the bedside table. Erica brought her magazines and Mrs Bunbury carried in a luncheon tray, soup and fish nicely cooked and served. Coco was taken to the kitchen to be fed and then came back and curled up on a rug, and Kerry lay in bed feeling helpless and rather silly.

There were callers to Maen Bos that afternoon. She could hear voices and footsteps in the hall. One voice belonged to Penny Penrose who said, 'Good heavens, fallen down again,' and probably summed up what most of them who had met Kerry were thinking, as though Kerry was perpetually off balance. Penny had been told about Coco and the mine. 'Naughty doggie,' she scolded, 'and you don't look a bit sorry. Doesn't he look as if he's smiling?'

During the afternoon there was a phone call from Louise who had gone round the little house in her lunch-hour and thought it was lovely. Kerry took the call on a plug-in phone and had to wait until Louise drew breath before she could say, 'I can't get back this weekend. You're not going to believe this but I've turned my ankle again and this time I've torn the ligament.'

'Oh dear.' Louise was all sympathy. 'Oh, I am sorry, Rob's going to be so upset. He's going to be sure it's all his fault.' She was as worried for Rob as she was for Kerry. 'Shall we come down and fetch you and bring your car back?'

'No, thank you,' said Kerry. 'I'm just not up to travelling right now.' That was true enough, and Louise said maybe the house would still be on the market when Kerry could get around again.

'Uhuh,' said Kerry and listened to footsteps crossing the hall that might have been David's. But if they were he didn't come into her room, and Louise said, 'Bye, then,' and Mrs Bunbury, who had brought in the phone, took it away.

Adrian returned home having heard nothing of the day's events. He had been out of town all day and he hurried to her bedside. She wasn't looking too bad now. She had made up her face and she was wearing a multi-coloured silk-fringed shawl, belonging to Erica, over her shoulders. 'How did it happen?' Adrian wanted to know. 'I thought your ankle was all right again.'

'Nearly, but not quite up to a second jolt, and it was rough down there.'

'Down where?' He hadn't waited to hear the details, and she started to tell him.

'Coco went down a shaft by the old mine and David and I went down to get him.'

'How far?'

She grimaced. 'It seemed miles to me. He'd run into the old flooded workings.'

'After the dog?' he gasped. 'You went down there after a dog?'

He thought they were mad, and there had been danger.

Adrian would not have risked it but David had acted coolly, breaking down the entrance, bringing the torch. At no time had David panicked.

'You think I should have left him?' she asked and he gave Coco a look of dislike.

'Yes, rather than have you risking your neck.'

'My neck's all right. It's my ankle I twisted.' Her smile was wry. 'If you'd been with me when I couldn't walk, would you have left me?'

'What a question! You know I wouldn't.' But he wouldn't have been with her. She couldn't see Adrian swimming through the black water, and she laughed softly and he said huffily, 'I don't find it funny. You know how I feel about you. You're precious and special, and I can't bear the thought of your being hurt.'

Didn't he realise that poor old Coco being buried alive would have hurt her a lot? But she said nothing and the evening wore on. Food was brought to her. Erica looked in constantly and Vicky from the Galleries was a caller and Adrian brought her a radio. He stayed for a while but he had to see someone on business so he couldn't spend all evening with Kerry, and around eleven o'clock he came to say good night.

She would feel better after a night's sleep, he assured her, but she was to stay where she was tomorrow. She knew this already and he kissed her cheek and said that Mrs Bunbury would be helping her get ready for the night. It was in fact Erica who arrived to give a supporting arm and when Kerry was back in bed, she asked, 'Now is there anything else you want?'

'Nothing else thank you,' said Kerry. 'Oh—er—is David here?'

'Yes.'

'Say good night to him for me. I'm going to read another chapter of this book. I've been here for hours so I'm not very tired.'

She had hoped she would have seen him before now. Coco had been removed from the room several times during the day and taken to the garden, and each time she had half expected David to come back with him. She had listened for his footsteps and strained to hear his voice, and he was in the house now and he wasn't bothering with her. But he might come if Erica said she had asked about him and she wasn't going to sleep right away. Just to say good night and talk for a few minutes.

She waited, hardly breathing, and when there was a tap on the door she knew that if it was anyone else she would be bitterly disappointed.

There was no sign that he had had a rough day, he looked immaculate, but the sight of him shocked her because she wanted so desperately to hold out her arms. She felt such a rush of longing that she dared not speak or move, and she sat smiling a tight-lipped smile, her fingers locked together.

He asked her if she was comfortable and what had happened to her lip. 'I chewed on it,' she said. 'It's puffed up since so now I've got a fat lip and a fat ankle. I wanted to tell you I'm sorry I'm stuck here and I can't go away on Saturday but you don't need to worry about Adrian.'

'No?'

'He's disappointed that I'm accident-prone. Rosalind never turned her ankle all the time she was rushing around the forest. She never even caught a cold. Anyhow, I'm not really accident-prone, I'm never ill and it's years since I had any trouble with this ankle, and this time I think it was the curse of the knackers.'

She was talking too much now. She wanted him to say 'Hush', sit down on the bed and take her in his arms. The words spoke themselves as she looked up at him. 'Will you kiss me good night?'

His lips were cool on her flushed cheek and she reached to hold his hand and beg, 'Stay and talk to me.'

'You've had enough bedtime stories for one day.' He could have been dealing with a child, but she was a woman, and she said abruptly,

'We weren't lovers, it was all play-acting.' When he didn't speak she asked, 'Don't you believe me?'

'I believe you.' But he didn't sound as though it mattered and she closed her eyes and asked, because she couldn't stop now,

'Do you—want me?'

'What man wouldn't?' She knew he was smiling and she thought she would have sold her soul to make him weep. 'But if you're looking for a father figure to keep you safe . . .' She felt his touch on her hair, brushing it back from her forehead, and her eyes opened wide. He shook his head. 'That's not me,' he said. At the door he asked, 'Shall I turn off the light?' and she said, 'Why not?'

The darkness seemed as choking as the blackness of the mine and she could not have felt more rejected if he had left her there. She clapped both her hands over her mouth because it would have done no good at all to start screaming, 'Come back.'

CHAPTER EIGHT

'I MADE such a fool of myself last night,' said Kerry, waking, sitting up, and addressing Coco who was still snoring on the rug. 'So did you yesterday,' she went on, 'but you weren't in my league.'

She spoke softly but aloud, trying to sound as though it was funny. Perhaps it was to David. There was something comic in being propositioned by someone who hadn't a hope. 'What man wouldn't?' he had said when she had asked him 'Do you want me?' and he had smiled and brushed her hair out of her eyes and said no-thank-you and left her.

The bit about a father figure was no excuse. He had kept her safe, he had looked after her, but there the burden had stopped. She was stuck for a few days but she did not need long-term protection. She was strong and smart. Up to a point she was smart, she hadn't been very smart last night. He knew she didn't see him as a father, she saw him as a lover, and the answer was still, 'Not me, lady.'

So he was right. If he felt that way it wouldn't work. She couldn't be one of the females who made all the running. She was sure Madeleine was. You only had to see them together, the way her eyes kept following him about, the way she kept touching him. And she might be able to paint balloons but she was a pain who didn't look as if she had ever really laughed in her life. So she must be fantastic in bed, and the jealousy hit Kerry like a blow in the face.

She lay back on the pillows after that, hot with fury. It was primitive, mindless, and if she didn't get it under control a night might soon come when she might drag herself upstairs to beat on David's door because she couldn't bear the thought of him being in there with Madeleine.

That would be the ultimate humiliation, after that she would cut her throat, so she mustn't even *think* of them together. And she must hold down this crazy longing for a man who didn't want her, because if she had any glimmer of hope of getting him it would be in his time. Slowly, slowly, even if she was burning. And the state she was in now she couldn't run after anybody.

The door opened and Erica walked in, wearing a white satin housecoat trimmed with swansdown and looking like somebody out of Dallas. 'Sleep well?' she asked. 'You're looking better,' and Kerry knew that her face was hot and lied,

'I'm feeling marvellous, I'm sure I could get up.'

Of course she couldn't. Erica was appalled at the suggestion, and the trip to the cloakroom proved her point because putting that foot to the floor took the flush from Kerry's face and left her pale.

After that she swallowed her pain-killers and lay still until Mrs Bunbury came in with a cup of tea and went off with Coco and the vase of fading roses.

She sipped the tea and wondered how she was going to face David. She hoped he wouldn't look in until she had had the chance to wash and put on some make-up. Seeing her sitting here, all mussed and miserable, he would find it incredible that she had fancied her chances against Madeleine. Madeleine Brenner was beautiful. Bitchy and boring, but beautiful, and trying not to think about her was like trying to keep the ankle still, an ache that flared into agony at every little jolt.

Kerry had never been jealous before, nor as helpless as this. She went on gulping down the hot tea, blinking because her lip smarted and so did her eyes and maybe the best thing she could do for the rest of this day would be to pull the sheets over her head, like the sleeping-bag in the counting-room, and shut out everything.

Only it wouldn't have shut out anybody. Certainly not Adrian and Erica who came in together so that she had to repeat for Adrian that she had slept well and felt better. And then Coco bounded in and David stood in the doorway and Adrian said, 'I'll bring you some more roses, and no thorns.'

He took one hand and Erica took the almost empty teacup from the other, and David said, 'Good morning.'

She wondered if it was the idea of Adrian picking roses for her without thorns, or the memory of last night that made David raise a quizzical eyebrow, and she said with frantic brightness, 'Good morning. I was a little feverish last night, I hope I didn't talk too much nonsense.'

Adrian and Erica looked blank, asking what did she mean? Of course she had talked no nonsense. David said nothing but his expression said that he knew what she meant and she looked across at the smile on Coco's face and thought, you're both laughing at me and I wish I could find it funny.

'What are you all doing today?' she asked, desperately making small talk.

Erica was due at the beauty parlour, although she was in full make-up and her hair was in its usual carefully dishevelled style. Adrian was off to the Galleries. David was working, and that reminded Adrian who asked, 'Did you make that sketch of Rosalind before the accident?'

'Yes,' he said, and Erica smiled.

'If you hadn't you'd still have the chance, she can't run away now.'

'Kerry can always run away,' said David and Kerry thought, wishful thinking? and said,

'Tell me how.' She hated being helpless and she sounded bitter.

'But not yet,' he said, 'so be a good child and keep your foot still.' She hated him calling her a child, she frowned as she spoke,

'It's a long time since I was a good child.'

'Or a rose without a thorn,' he said. 'Do you want the morning paper?' He was carrying one which he put down on the bedside table. Not a newspaper she would have chosen but containing enough reading to last her for hours. Then he went and she wanted to call, 'When will you be back?' She didn't because it would have been the nearest thing to running after him, and Adrian said,

'I'll be back this afternoon,' and kissed her cheek, perhaps her bruised lip put him off, and she said, 'Don't worry; and don't hurry, I'm fine.'

'There's my brave girl.' He looked and sounded as if she was lying here with some terrible illness and she asked ruefully, 'What's brave about it?'

Erica reminded her that if there was anything she wanted she was to ring the dragon bell, and then she was on her own and all she wanted was to make herself presentable and for David to come back.

With Mrs Bunbury's help she managed the first and sat up in bed wearing a little make-up and with her tousled hair brushed. She had dressed to the extent of changing her nightgown for a bra, pants and shirt; no longer looking like an invalid made her feel better. And then she ate a little breakfast and read some of the newspaper David had left for her and most of the local paper that Mrs Bunbury brought in with the breakfast tray.

She went through the houses-for-sale pages looking for Penlyn properties and found a terraced house and a bungalow, in either of which she could have put up holiday-makers. She looked at Situations Vacant, although with luck she might be allowed to help out in the Galleries and do some secretarial work for Erica, especially if the Little Theatre went ahead.

She had to get out of Maen Bos but she desperately wanted to stay near, because this was where David Caradoc was and she knew for sure that anywhere else she would be lonely. Even if she didn't buy a house right away she could rent reasonably over the winter months.

When she came to Penlyn she had had no plans but now her immediate future seemed clear, and perhaps the pain-killers were making her euphoric because she could not believe that David could not feel the current of awareness between them. He hadn't given much sign of being affected by it up to now, but to Kerry it was electric.

Mrs Bunbury brought her white vellum notepaper carrying the Maen Bos address and she wrote to the friends who were storing her furniture, and others with whom she had been staying in Stowe, to explain about her ankle. She said she hoped to see them before long. Then she wrote to Ruth and said that the Little Theatre seemed quite a likely prospect and described how Coco had run into a mine shaft and how she and David had gone to get him out. But she didn't say much about David and nothing about the black water. Just that they had found the dog, and coming out she had manged to turn her ankle yet again and was now taking it easy in style in the Chinese room.

David didn't come back, but Madeleine turned up. The door was open and she walked in. The light caught her fall of dark smooth hair and it shone like satin, and her smoky blue eyes were distinctly unfriendly. 'You look comfortable,' she said, making it sound like an accusation. 'What's the role today? Little Orphan Annie?'

For a moment Kerry wondered if David had told her about Kerry's father, but it was more likely that she was referring to Kerry once more helpless, and needing care. 'I thought it was too good to be true,' she drawled, 'you leaving tomorrow. How long is it going to be this time?'

'No longer than I can help,' said Kerry, and Madeleine's eyes flickered over the letter she was writing, and the addressed envelopes on the bedside table.

'Invitations to the wedding?'

'Of course not.'

'Poor Adrian,' said Madeleine, 'he does get carried away.'

Kerry couldn't have agreed more but she wasn't saying so. Madeleine had only looked in to make herself objectionable, and Kerry said, 'Don't let me keep you.'

Mrs Bunbury came into the room with a glass of something to get down the mid-day pain-killers and Madeleine swept past her and Kerry said gratefully, 'Thank you.'

'It's fresh lemonade,' said Mrs Bunbury. 'Just squeezed.'

'I feel awful lying here making extra work.'

'It's nice to be thanked,' said Mrs Bunbury graciously. 'It's nice to be appreciated.' She looked towards the doorway through which Madeleine had just swanned. 'Unlike some,' she said darkly, 'who'd walk all over you. If that young madam ever gets to be Mrs David——' She shook her head and Kerry gulped and asked,

'Do you think she's likely to?'

Mrs Bunbury went on shaking her head but she wasn't saying no, just registering disapproval. Madeleine had probably been here all night, and now she was probably off to find David while Kerry was supposed to lie here all day and Kerry was suddenly seized with a fierce impatience. 'I'm getting awfully bored,' she said. 'If you could find me a walking-stick I'm sure I could get around.' She would put no weight on her foot, she wasn't that stupid, and after a moment Mrs Bunbury said, 'I might find you something better than a stick.'

Kerry had had a few minutes to ponder on that when she heard squeaking wheels coming down the hall and Mrs Bunbury pushed an old wickerwork bathchair into the room. 'I've dusted it,' she announced, 'and it needed oiling. It's been up in the attics but it seems sound enough.'

Kerry could imagine some Victorian or Edwardian lady, rug over her knees, being pushed around in this. She said, 'It's a collector's piece.' But in a houseful of collector's pieces that didn't impress Mrs Bunbury who wheeled it up to the bedside and explained, 'You can get along, pushing the wheels with your hands. On the flat, of course,' and Kerry hid a smile and wondered if Mrs Bunbury thought she was likely to try going up and down stairs. She really could have got herself a reputation for being accident-prone.

But the hall was quite a big area; there were rooms leading off, and she said, 'I'll be very careful and I'd love to try it,' and Mrs Bunbury draped a blanket over the chair and helped Kerry into a wrap-around skirt and one shoe.

Coco was suspicious about the squeaking, and kept sniffing the wickerwork and looking for mice as Kerry eased herself in. She tried not to giggle because Mrs Bunbury was very serious, pushing her out of the bedroom and taking a turn around the hall, while Kerry got the feel of it.

The wheels were stiff, the chair jerked at first when she tried to propel it herself, making her wince, but with a little practice she was moving smoothly enough and when Erica returned home about an hour later Kerry was making a very slow tour of the ground floor.

Erica was very taken with the bathchair. She hadn't even known it was in the attics. She examined it with as much interest as Coco, and Kerry was sure she was imagining herself being wheeled around, looking pale and interesting—but not ill, of course.

Adrian thought she should have stayed where the doctor told her. He came back to Maen Bos in the late afternoon when Kerry was sitting at a window in the drawing-room and his first comment was, 'You shouldn't be out of bed, you're supposed to be resting your foot.'

'I'm using my hands, not my feet,' she said.

'What happens if you tip out of that contraption?'

'I won't.' She moved to show him it was stable, backing away from the window and through the open door into the hall. Then she saw David crossing and called, 'Hi!'

'Making a bolt for it?' he asked.

'I shall need a bit more practice. I can't turn round the corners yet.' She heard Adrian sigh as if her zaniness irritated him. She had warned him he didn't know the first thing about her, but he still thought she should be playing Rosalind.

That evening Adrian had another shock. So did Kerry, although she should have been prepared. David had not been in the house all evening. It seemed he had an exhibition in New York at the end of the year and he was working towards that. Kerry wondered if Madeleine was keeping him company in the studio but she couldn't ask, and she ate with Erica and Adrian and then sat with Erica watching television. The pain-killers were working but they made her slightly drowsy and when Adrian came into the room she was just about ready to ask if she might go to bed.

Adrian's excuse for not being with them had been VAT returns but he came in carrying a big white sheet of cartridge paper and frowning. He showed it to his mother and asked, 'What do you think of that?' and Kerry thought it might be either the knackers or her own portrait, and when Erica said, 'Oh,' sounding disappointed, it wasn't hard to guess which. 'It's very good, I suppose,' said Erica grudgingly, 'but it isn't how I see you.'

'I don't think it's a good likeness at all,' Adrian grumbled, and Kerry had to ask, 'May I?' before he showed it to her.

She had known it wouldn't be flattering but she could never complain that David had made her plain. It was quite striking. She lounged in the chair, boyish in jeans and jacket, and it was a strong face, tough, modern.

'I don't think it's like you at all,' Adrian repeated and she said ruefully,

'Oh, but it is.' Sometimes. The young thug, how David had first seen her and still did. It was a portrait to disillusion Adrian all right. He could never imagine this girl was a rose without a thorn, and now he was looking at Kerry as though he was seeking a resemblance.

'I don't think I want it,' he said at last and Kerry almost said, 'Of course you don't, I told you all along.' 'Would you mind if I went to bed?' she asked, instead.

The night was not good. Her leg hurt when she tossed as she lay trying to sleep, and wondering what was happening in this great house. Wondering, that was what was happening with David. He had tapped on her door when it was almost midnight and her bedside lamp was still burning, looking in when she called, 'Come in,' but only to ask, 'All right?'

She told him, 'Adrian doesn't like the sketch.'

'So he said.'

'You made me look a very tough case.'

'Aren't you?' he said, and laughed and went away.

But she was not, and that was why she suffered not knowing if Madeleine was here. Once she could get about she would know and it would be easier to face, but now she was helpless, and she wondered if he had not come into her room tonight because of last night.

She wanted him as she had never wanted any other

man. He had never taken her seriously but she was falling more and more deeply in love with him, and once she was fit again she would get through that self-control of his and under his skin no matter what she had to do.

She dreamed of the things she would do and it all seemed possible, as if the first word and the first caress would unlock such a passionate response that she could give all of herself completely and gloriously. But that was dreaming. When she lay awake she thought he might never need anything from her, always be unreachable.

She could be left carrying a torch for him, and what the hell did that mean? Burning up inside until you turned into ashes? It could happen. She could be that obsessed. In the dark of the night she was terrified of the power he exerted over her, without trying or caring.

By daylight she was at least in control of herself. She trundled around in her bathchair and talked with callers to Maen Bos, friends of Erica's who came to lunch.

The pain-killers were sedatives, and although Kerry had halved the dosage today she did spend some time dozing on her bed. Adrian went to call on a buyer who was in the market for eighteenth-century etchings of the district, a collection of which had turned up in a house sale last week. And David was working in the studio in the garden, she didn't see him all day.

In the evening three bridge players arrived and they and Erica made a foursome at a bridge table at the far end of the drawing-room. Adrian and a bunch of local artists, and Kerry on the sofa again, were a small party at the other end of the room.

They drank wine and the others talked about their work and their colleagues. Some of it was terribly intense and some was bitchy and some was quite witty, and Kerry could have slipped into the jargon and been one of them but she was miles away in her mind. She looked as if she was listening, she acted interest, while the voices droned on and nothing really reached her.

Then David walked in and it was like waking up from dozing. And she wasn't the only one who felt that way. His dynamism affected them all. He was the master, the artist with genius, and also, she thought wryly, the sexiest man in the room. His physical presence sent the vibes buzzing, and Kerry watched the women perking up and smiling and wiped the smile off her own face, so that when he looked across at her she looked a little bored. Soon after she excused herself and went to bed and thought, I can't stay on here much longer.

There was a letter from Louise in the mail next morning containing the estate agent's leaflet about the house in Stowe, which Louise still imagined Kerry might buy. Rob sent his love, he had been shattered to hear about the ankle giving way again and he and a mate were prepared to drive down and bring Kerry and her car, still in the Wayside car park, back to Stowe.

Kerry phoned Wayside that morning and talked to Mrs Hayle, telling her that Coco was fine and asking was there any chance that she could move back into Wayside with him in a few more days. She wouldn't be walking well, but she would be walking by then, and then she could set about looking at local property. Mrs Hayle said there would be a room and Kerry put down the phone with her bolt-hole assured for when she needed it.

That was rather sooner than she expected. Wednesday afternoon, to be exact. Everybody was nice to her here. No one suggested she was outstaying her welcome. Erica was happily involved in her plans for a little theatre. Kerry was making all sorts of notes about that, and typing letters for Erica who was enjoying having her own personal secretary to hand. Adrian picked roses for her and spent every evening at home, and was charming and chatty about his day in the Galleries. But he looked thoughtful, Kerry thought, and she knew that David's sketch of her had taken the rose-coloured spectacles from his eyes. Adrian was seeing her in a different light now, the dream was ending for him and she was glad about that.

Her own dream should have been fading too, because although she saw quite a lot of David he was not falling for her. He liked her, he didn't mind her convalescing in Maen Bos, but never once did he look at her as if he wanted to make love to her. When he was near she ached for him, and even when they were apart she carried him with her. She could never entirely forget him. It was terrible, acting all the time, straining to be cool, smiling and confident, while she was silently crying out for love.

By Wednesday afternoon she was out of the bathchair, getting around with a stick but keeping her injured foot rigid. She was in the Chinese room, writing to Louise, when Madeleine walked in. Kerry hadn't seen Madeleine since Saturday, although that didn't mean she hadn't been in the house.

'So you're still here,' said Madeleine and there was no answer to that until she asked, 'Why?'

Then Kerry shrugged. 'Because nobody's told me to go yet.'

'You might as well,' said Madeleine. 'Adrian's having second thoughts. When anyone asks him now when the wedding's going to be he says there's nothing settled.'

'Does he?' Kerry murmured, and Madeleine said primly, 'I'd have more pride than to hang around when a man doesn't want me.'

'Would you?' said Kerry, and thought, you do, you do, I'm almost sure that you do; and snapped, 'There never was anything settled, it was all nonsense,' and Madeleine looked vacant with surprise.

'Then why——' she began. And stopped, and stared, and said slowly and incredulously, 'It couldn't be? *No!* It couldn't be because of *David*?'

'It could not,' said Kerry, but her face was flaming and she heard herself prattling about the little theatre, and she heard Madeleine start laughing. She had seen Madeleine smirk, heard her little trills of laughter, but this time Madeleine fairly screeched.

Even the dog was looking at her, wondering what the noise was about. 'But that would be hysterical,' she gasped. 'There've always been sex-starved girls panting for David, but an *actress*! After years of Erica don't you think he's about had enough of actresses? If you've any ideas there——' She made a dismissive gesture, waving a hand, wiping them out. 'Not a chance,' she said.

Kerry had been wrong, Madeleine did have a sense of humour, she thought this was screamingly funny. And after twenty years of Erica who was always acting, living the life of high drama, it was ridiculous to think that David might take on another 'star who didn't make it'. He had said that once. An actress would have a hard time convincing him that her feelings were more than skin-deep. He would never completely trust an actress.

'Of course I am an artist, as he is,' said Madeleine smugly. 'We talk the same language. We have a real understanding that goes beyond sex. I never intrude. I appreciate he needs space and solitude to do his own thing, he has such immense talent. But he values my advice and my opinions because he knows that I am a free spirit as he is.'

'Oh, go paint a balloon,' said Kerry wearily, and Madeleine raised her smoothly arched brows and looked down her almost perfect nose and said,

'You're jealous of my talent, of course. It happens all the time. And I can understand you getting a crush on David, that happens all the time too, but I do think you'd be happier if you went home.'

'I'm going,' said Kerry. 'It's just the ankle that's holding me back and you must admit there's always a laugh where Erica is.'

After Madeleine had gone Kerry sat thinking. Madeleine Brenner was malicious, but she was an artist and Adrian said her work was well thought of, so she had that in common with David. Her work was an asset while Kerry's gifts were a definite liability, and the longer Kerry stayed in Maen Bos the more he would look on her as a second Erica. She was turning into Erica's understudy with all these plans for the little theatre. In Wayside she could be herself, she could plan from there, decide on her next move, and she wouldn't lie awake at night because somewhere above her head David and Madeleine might be sleeping together.

I want out, she decided, and slowly she packed her bag. She would ask David to drive her down to Wayside. Why not? Adrian wasn't here and neither was Erica, and if Madeleine was sharing the studio Madeleine could see her off too.

But she would tell David she was going and wait for a flicker of regret in his expression and for the very faint hope that he might say, 'Why? You can stay here as long as you like.'

It wasn't far, from the house through the little spinney to reach the lawn where the changing-tent had been pitched and where the studio stood. But it was farther than she had walked with this torn ligament, and she debated whether to get back into the bathchair. In the end she decided it would be awkward manoeuvring that between trees and over turf, so she stepped out with her walking-stick and with Coco, who never left her.

Mrs Bunbury was in the house, so was the woman who came in from Penlyn to help with the housework, and there was usually someone working in the gardens. But this afternoon Kerry saw nobody. She went carefully, taking no risks, passing the back of the summer arbour. If David was not in the studio this would be a wasted trip and she would sit down on the grass and rest before she turned back for the house. While she was resting she would be waiting because she wanted to tell him first that she was leaving, and she knew how much she was gambling on him stopping her.

If he was working and if he was alone he might resent an interruption. Madeleine never intruded. She understood that he needed solitude because she was another free spirit. 'She's an idiot,' said Kerry to Coco, 'why shouldn't we intrude on him? He intrudes on me. He never gives me a minute's peace.'

Coco frolicked around the lawn, and the door to the studio was open a little and if there was nobody there she would go inside and wait. When she was near enough she shouted 'Anybody in?' and leaned against a tree.

David came to the door, wearing a grey polo-necked sweater and grey slacks. There was grey clay on his hands and she thought crazily, well he's working, not making love to Madeleine with hands in that state. 'Should you be out here?' he said.

'I'm a very tough case. I'm managing.' But now she was here her leg was aching. 'What I came to ask you,' she said, 'was, did you bring my knackers sketch from the mine?'

'No.'

'Oh! Because I would like it and if it were here I could pack it and take it with me.'

He didn't say stay, he said, 'If you do want it I can fetch it for you.'

'Only I am going this afternoon.'

'I won't be a minute.' He left her leaning against the tree, wishing she had come in the bathchair so that she could have set off fast away from here. There was no way he was stopping her leaving Maen Bos, he was practically helping her to pack. He didn't give a damn, but when he was near she wanted his arms around her so badly that her mind spun out of control. She stood where she was, watching the open door of the studio, and wondering if she was a good enough actress to go on smiling or if any moment now she was going to crack up.

He came out quite soon and shut the door behind him. There was no clay on his hands now and he said, 'I can leave the work for a while, I've wrapped it.'

She echoed, 'Wrapped it?' and he explained, 'In a wet cloth and covered with a plastic sheet. Or it would crack, fall apart.'

'Fancy,' she said, and thought, somebody should do that to me, to stop me falling apart, and she asked brightly, 'Are you going to fetch my sketch now? How kind of you.'

'Will you come?'

'Tough I may be but I'm not quite up to hobbling over the hills.'

'Then it's the bathchair or the Range Rover,' he said, and she wanted to laugh to show she could always see a joke but she said 'The Range Rover' quickly because it wasn't going to be a joke. She was going with him because the counting-house, by the mine, was where they had been closest. No one would walk in on them there. Not Madeleine, nor Erica. 'So I'm going this afternoon,' she might say, 'but not too far away, and have you ever stopped to think that your Madeleine is a right twit?' If she drank another half-tumbler of that whisky she would say something like that.

He left her sitting on the white marble steps that led up to the summerhouse, down which she had walked as Rosalind that first afternoon. She had looked for him then, in the audience. 'Is yonder the man?' she had said, and fixed her eyes on Rob. But she had seen David and her voice had caught in her throat.

It was the man, heaven help her. From then on he had been the man, and all her struggles, all her defensiveness, had still brought her to this in the end. Sitting on the steps waiting for him, and knowing he would never wait for her any time or any place.

The car came through the archway in the hedge. He drove it straight across the lawn, and she got up as he opened the passenger door and took his hand to haul herself in. Coco followed and squirmed over on to the back seat where he sat, looking out on the gardens.

They came through the lawn of the standing stones and she asked, 'Are these good? I mean, I wouldn't know. What would you call them? Natural sculptures?'

'Very nice rocks,' he said.

'Was he a good artist?'

David smiled. 'He was a great talker about his art. Not a great artist but a great talker.'

'Sounds like Madeleine,' she muttered and she went on because she was so screwed up with nerves that silence would have been unendurable. 'This exhibition of yours in New York, where's it being held?'

'At the Felix Klopper Galleries,' he said.

'Is *that* good?' Of course she didn't know and of course it would be, and she went on asking questions. What was he showing? Where were they coming from? Would the Tin Miner be making the trip? How about the piece he had just wrapped in a damp cloth?

The car bounded along the old road, faster than their last trip, but not much, and when Coco saw something that started him barking she asked, 'Is the mine shaft blocked up?'

'Walled up.'

'Because I don't think I could face that again. In a hundred years' time an archaeologist could find your shirt down there. Unless the knackers have found it. If the knacker girls are handy with their needles they could get three or four little shirts out of it for two-foot-high men.'

That was when she realised what drivel she was talking, and after that she looked out of the window, and said hardly anything until they reached the top of the hill, overlooking the ruins of the mine.

The drive had shaken her. It would have been easier if she had been able to relax but sitting beside him had kept her stiff as a poker, and she opened the door as the car drew up and almost toppled out.

That was the last thing she wanted to do, fall awkwardly and twist another muscle. She steadied herself and climbed down and leaned on her stick and said, 'I can manage.' But he took her arm and then she leaned on him while he unlocked the counting-house door. Then she limped in and sat in the straightbacked chair.

Now she was here she didn't know what to do. She wanted to be bright and beautiful, very very sexy but not too pushy, because this was only a beginning. All she hoped for was to make him look at her differently, and admit the power of the physical attraction between them. He *must* feel it too, but she couldn't tell him she was in love with him. That would be asking too much.

Coco had followed her in. Now he trotted towards the open door and David said, 'Not this time,' and closed the door and she asked,

'Where's my picture?'

He opened the cupboard. It was rolled up, a white tube on a shelf, and when he handed it to her and she unrolled it the funny little sketches made her smile although she wanted to cry. Suppose this was all she was left with? He was looking down at her and she said, 'Could I have a cup of coffee? Could I have the sleeping-bag to sit on?'

'Of course.' The sleeping-bag was rolled up in there. He unrolled it and she got off the wooden chair. Coco joined her on the sleeping-bag and David filled a kettle from the plastic water container, lit a cigar and sat down in the wooden armchair, the other side of the big table.

She remembered the last time she had seen him smoking, the aroma of the smoke curling up from the ashtray, and David saying, 'Don't imagine you've stumbled into Camelot or the Forest of Arden.'

He must have guessed what she was thinking because he said, 'Only in times of stress.'

'Like the night Adrian said he was going to marry me?'

'I walked outside that night and watched your window. When your light went on I came in. I thought you were going to his room.'

She had thought it was coincidence, she hadn't realised she was under supervision, and she said wryly, 'And told me about the money and warned me off. Well, I can see where the stress was then.'

'I doubt it,' he said. 'I couldn't let you marry Adrian because I wanted you myself.'

It *had* been the same for him, the sexual attraction together with the antagonism and the laughter. She knew that soon he would put out that cigar and come over to her and she said, 'Well, I offered.'

'With a cut lip and a wrenched ankle and doctor's orders to lie still. You must have known you were safe enough. And you did say next morning you'd been talking rubbish.'

They were both smiling but when he stood up her heart leapt in her chest like a caged thing. This was what she wanted more than anything in the world, but her heart beat fast because once she let him make love to her it would mean her complete surrender. She could never pretend with him again, and she stared at him with wide eyes.

But he didn't come to her. He opened the drawer and took out two more sketches which he laid on the table top, and when he looked at her this time he was not smiling. He said, 'Don't buy that house in Stowe. When

you stayed before and I asked you why, I hoped you
might say "Because of you" but of course you didn't. This
time I'm asking you, please don't go.'

She was dumbstruck. She knew what she had heard,
but she could not take in the fact that he could not face a
parting any more than she could, although she hadn't
been going back to Stowe, only to Wayside.

He brought the two sketches, handing them down to
her where she sat on the sleeping-bag. They were both of
her, and good likenesses just as the one he had done for
Adrian had been. But these were different. In one she
slept, her face cushioned by the sleeping-bag, looking
young and vulnerable. The second showed her waking, a
half-smile on her lips, and her eyes were those of a
woman looking up at the man with whom she shares
everything that makes life wonderful.

Maybe she had looked like that, waking in here, when
David touched her and she opened her eyes and saw him.
She whispered, 'Did I look like that?'

'No,' he said. 'But I want you to wake beside me and
look at me that way.'

When he made love to her she would look at him with
that complete and radiant commitment, but for now she
couldn't raise her head and she heard herself ask, 'You
don't think I'm a second Erica?'

'You're a better actress, and you're like her in no other
way. I soon realised that.'

'But you're fond of Erica?' Nervousness was keeping
her chattering.

'Very,' he said, 'although she's absurd and amoral and
hopelessly extravagant.'

'Amoral? She has affairs?'

'Most of the time.' He sounded as he usually did when
he spoke of Erica, tolerant and amused. 'But recently
she's had the Flower Festival and now she's full of this
idea of a little theatre.' He added, 'And Adrian is very

much her son, equally susceptible.'

'So I noticed.'

'But I think he would have settled for Rosalind.'

'I wouldn't,' she said. 'They both fall in love easily, do they?' Not deeply but easily.

'Yes.'

'You don't?'

'No.'

She loved him. It was not only a physical hunger, although that raged through every cell of her body. But she wanted him in every way. Waking and sleeping, in sickness and health. She wanted to share her life with him, grow old with him.

He wanted to make love to her, although he had not said he loved her, and she said wistfully, 'You never gave much sign of fancying me.'

His grin was rueful. 'If it interests you I've had the greatest difficulty keeping my hands off you ever since you fell down the stairs. That made me realise how much you meant to me. I never wanted to take any woman from a man before but I wanted to snatch you out of Adrian's arms when he picked you up.'

'Did you think we were lovers?'

'I suppose I did,' he said. 'After that dinner-party when you were upstairs together, that disturbed me, made me angry. It made me jealous although I didn't realise it at the time. I didn't want to think about it.'

She said suddenly and fiercely, 'You slept with Madeleine,' and he said,

'Not after you came.'

Coco was lying, nose on paws. As though he sensed something electric charging the atmosphere, his head jerked from girl to man.

She said, 'I might have had an affair with Adrian, I was lonely and unhappy enough when I came down here, but I didn't. You kept getting in the way. You do have that effect on me. You manage to block other things out. Other men too.'

'That's a good start,' he said, 'because from that first night I haven't been able to get you out of my mind, whatever I was doing.' He spoke in his usual quiet deep voice. 'I want you to stay here. That's why I've let Erica start on the coach-house conversion, to keep you near. When you asked me if I wanted you I knew it wasn't a serious question but the answer is—as I have never wanted any other woman. You are the one and I can wait. I'll block out the other men, I promise you that, but I can wait as long as I have to because some time we shall come together. And stay together because you are going to need me as much as I need you.'

The cigar smoked in a saucer and he said, 'Stay with me and try to get used to the idea.'

As he got up to take off the boiling kettle she said, 'I think I love you.'

'What?' he said 'What?'

She knew she loved him, that there could never be any other man for her. He was prepared to woo her, to seduce her gently and patiently, and maybe she should settle for that at least until her ankle mended.

But she ached for him and she said, 'You could help me make up my mind. Or would that be taking an unfair advantage because I still can't run?'

He came and sat beside her, taking her hands, and she almost pulled away in a reflex of tension. Then he drew her into his arms and she looked up into his face, seeing the strength of it, the male sensuality, and knew that this man could lift her to undreamed-of heights of ecstasy. He could carry her through the stars, blow her to pieces, and her lips parted in a soft cry.

'Hush, my love, my sweet love,' he said, and he kissed her, a long slow kiss. She melted, falling back, letting his mouth take hers, letting his tongue make love to hers, tasting joy.

Her shirt slipped from her shoulders. She did none of it. She lay supine, as the light touch of his fingers sent little electric thrills through her. Firm fingers were massaging the back of her neck, and all the time he kissed her, caressed her. And her own passion grew, shaking her like strong hands, until her body was screaming for him, for the smell and taste and feel of his skin and the hardness of him.

She never knew when she took over, if she ever did. Or if she was drawn into the age-old rhythm of taking and giving, moving together, in a lovemaking that made them one and made her his. And yet she always knew that this man was with her, part of her, holding her, leading her. This was love and it burst on her, ecstatic and endless, and she was in a million pieces; but she floated down with his arms still around her, and she was not alone, she was with him for ever.

But incredibly, long afterwards—she slept, she was sure she did, in the circle of his arms. When she looked up at him he was looking down at her and the hard face was naked and vulnerable, as if he were waiting to hear something that mattered terribly to him. She had never seen David Caradoc like this, and she knew that nobody had, and she knew how much she meant to him.

'I love you more than life,' he said. I love you, she was going to say, but he went on, 'So will you tell that dog we're getting married right away?'

Coco grinned, as he always did, and Kerry sat up, her bare shoulders gleaming in the light that filtered through the windows. She looked at the man beside her, at the blaze of love in his eyes, and knew that her whole world was here.

'You heard the man,' she said.

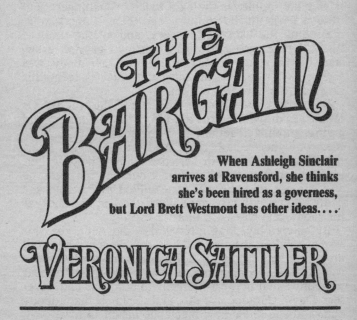

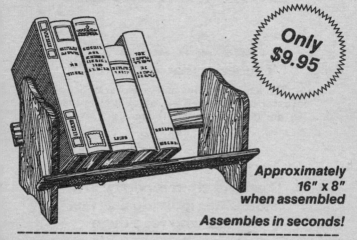

Six exciting series for you every month... from Harlequin

Harlequin Romance·
The series that started it all

Tender, captivating and heartwarming...
love stories that sweep you off to faraway places
and delight you with the magic of love.

Harlequin Presents·
Powerful contemporary love stories...as individual as the women who read them

The No. 1 romance series...
exciting love stories for you, the woman of today...
a rare blend of passion and dramatic realism.

Harlequin Superromance®
It's more than romance...
it's Harlequin Superromance

A sophisticated, contemporary romance-fiction
series, providing you with a longer,
more involving read...a richer mix of complex plots,
realism and adventure.

Harlequin
American Romance™
Harlequin celebrates the American woman...

...by offering you romance stories written about American women, by American women for American women. This series offers you contemporary romances uniquely North American in flavor and appeal.

◆

Harlequin Temptation™
Passionate stories for today's woman

An exciting series of sensual, mature stories of love...dilemmas, choices, resolutions... all contemporary issues dealt with in a true-to-life fashion by some of your favorite authors.

◆

Harlequin Intrigue
Because romance can be quite an adventure

Harlequin Intrigue, an innovative series that blends the romance you expect... with the unexpected. Each story has an added element of intrigue that provides a new twist to the Harlequin tradition of romance excellence.

Harlequin Books·

Harlequin Romance

Coming Next Month

Available in December wherever paperback books are sold, or through Harlequin Reader Service.

In the U.S.
901 Fuhrmann Blvd.
P.O. Box 1397
Buffalo, N.Y. 14240-1397

In Canada
P.O. Box 603
Fort Erie, Ontario
L2A 5X3